Terra Cotta Beauty

Live beautifully
Live passionately
Learn wisely
JN

Jola Naibi

Jola Naibi
P.O. Box 1683
Bowie, MD, 20717
USA.
www.jolanaibi.com

The characters and events in this publication are fictitious. Any resemblance to real
persons (living or dead) or real events is purely coincidental
Printed in the United States of America
Library of Congress Cataloguing in Publication Data
ISBN: 1491271671
ISBN 13: 9781491271674
Library of Congress Control Number: 2014901216
CreateSpace Independent Publishing Platform
North Charleston, South Carolina
Cover illustration

Dedicated to the exceptionally wonderful memory of Oluremi Johnson (née Caxton-Naibi), whose studious example continues to serve as an inspiration

I had been raised to believe that time delivers our dreams
and quietly carries our nightmares away, and that most
of what lies ahead is welcoming and serene.

Thomas McGuane
Driving on the Rim (2010)

Acknowledgements

*A*lthough they are all completely fictional, the stories in Terra-Cotta Beauty are a reflection of some of the personal stories that I encountered as a young adult in Lagos. The winds of life have carried me to so many places but my heart still remains back home.

When I lived in Lagos, my friend Sola saw something in me that took me a while to discover in myself and I am heartily thankful that our paths crossed, without that first ever so slight hint of encouragement, I do not think I would have had the courage to write.

I cherish the friendship that I would later develop with Linda. I met her at a time in my life which I call the '*Should I? Shouldn't I? Am I? Aren't I*' phase of my life, as I went through a period of self-discovery. We started our own two-person book club, during which I was introduced to authors who remained solidly loyal to their roots while their feet were planted in the diaspora – Tan, Lahiri, Lapcharoensap. Their writings would influence mine.

Some of the stories in Terra-Cotta Beauty were first brought to life on a blog that I called *La Racontrice* (The Female Story Teller) and I am thankful for the support and encouragement that I received from my fellow bloggers especially those who took the time to provide constructive criticism on my writing – Naapali, Ms. Catwalq, Omohemi Benson, Atutupoyoyo, Solomonsydelle, Kiibaati, Olu, Omosewa, laspapi, Favoured Girl, Imnakoya, Kiibaati and Noni Moss. Thank you guys. Even as I navigated through the magical maze of writing and self-publishing, I could see you all cheering me from the sidelines.

Contents

Ol' Boi

They had lived on that street for as long as he could remember. It was a short street that ended in a T shape at a cement wall that shielded the backyard of another compound on another street. Everyone in the entire neighborhood dumped their rubbish at this end of the street. Very rarely the authorities would clear the trash, but most of the time there was a huge pile of garbage at the end of the street, which stunk like rotten eggs. The wind, especially the light wind of the morning, often carried the smell across the whole street and beyond. Most mornings, on their way out, they would see people with their palms across their faces, trying to shield themselves from the choking smell. Even with the car windows all the way up, they still got a good whiff of it.

Their house was a light brown duplex at the very beginning of the street with two large iron double gates and a smaller gate attached to it. Visitors to the house would first encounter the guard, whom everyone called Mallam. Mallam had many friends, who often congregated in front of the residence at all hours of the day, chatting and listening to a small transistor radio while seated on brightly colored mats on the concrete floor inside the gate of the house. Mallam and his friends often ate and prayed together, bowing and kneeling on the mats while facing the northeast wall of the compound. Visitors who came to the house by car would be let in through the large iron double gates by Mallam and have to park their vehicles behind their father's car, the only car on the premises. Visitors who came on foot would have to walk through the smaller gate past the gatehouse, a square-shaped room built into the wall surrounding the compound. The wall itself was about fifteen feet high and had pieces of broken glass embedded

1

into the cement on top of it. This was meant to be a security deterrent to prevent diehards from jumping over the wall and looting the house, but if you were dexterous and desperate enough, the broken glass and the height would not stop you.

The house itself was about twenty feet from the gatehouse. There were two apartments in the two-story building, one on each floor. They lived on the top floor, and their downstairs neighbor was the widow Mama Sholanke, who lived alone. She had lost her husband in a car accident years ago, and all her children were married and lived elsewhere. Their upstairs apartment had a balcony jutting out of the front of the house, and if you stood opposite the front windows of Mama Sholanke's apartment, you would be directly underneath the balcony of their apartment.

One night he had a dream that he had somehow fallen through the floor of the upstairs balcony and landed on his feet right opposite Mama's window. The following morning he woke up, excitedly jumped out of bed, and ran onto the balcony, where he jumped as hard as he could. He was surprised when nothing happened.

To get to their apartment, visitors would have to walk up two small steps through a wooden door, where they would come to a flight of stairs. To the right was the door to Mama Sholanke's apartment. The door was decorated with colorful stickers bearing different inscriptions: *Christ Evangelical Church, Angels on Guard, John 3:12, His Banner Over Us Is Love.* The wooden door at the top of the stairs led to their small three-bedroom apartment, which was shielded by a black iron gate. The front door of the apartment opened into the living room, and to the right were French windows, which led onto the balcony. They were usually opened during the day and closed at night because of mosquitoes.

The house was owned by Alhaji Adisa. The little boy and his sisters had never seen him because he lived on another side of the city, but the family was often visited by his son, Uncle Shamsudeen. Tomi, the baby of the family, could not pronounce his name and called him Uncle Sardine. They all found this funny, including Uncle Sardine, such that anytime he came over he would tap lightly on the door and say in a large, booming voice, "It is me, your Uncle Sardine!"

He came to visit them once a month, and he would sit in the living room drinking Fanta Orange with their father—no matter how many times his host offered it to him coaxingly, Uncle Sardine never touched alcohol. He and their father would engage in a series of discussions that would touch on a range of issues, from football to the state of the nation. During the Muslim holidays, Uncle Sardine would bring them huge chunks of raw lamb meat wrapped in blood-stained old newspapers. The little boy noticed that each time Uncle Sardine visited, his father would go into his bedroom and come back with a bulging envelope, which he handed to him, while the latter would bow his head in thanks and leave shortly after. When he left he would hear his father sigh loudly. On the day it happened, his mother and two sisters had decided to have their hair done at the salon two streets down. He had no interest in going with them. Although he had been there a couple of times, he often felt out of place in the midst of all those women and girls. He also knew that his older sister, Tolu, would use the opportunity to tease him, but Tomi, his little baby sister, who was just three years old, would be happy to have him along and would even let him hold her hand as they walked. From the balcony he watched them leave through the pedestrian gate, craning his neck to see them disappear down the road.

His father came out to the balcony with a bottle of Star beer in one hand and a clean glass in the other. He sat in the cane chair just behind his son and poured the contents of the bottle into the glass. The young boy watched as the white foam rose above the gold liquid, while his father leaned back into the chair to relax. A light wind blew, bringing with it the fetid odor of the putrefying waste from the rubbish dump at the end of the street. The little boy wrinkled his nose as the waft hit his olfactory lobes, and he tried to preoccupy himself with the Voltron toy that his friend Bamidele had let him borrow. He could only play with it when his mother was out because she would skin him alive if she found out that he had borrowed a toy.

It was the middle of the afternoon, and they had had a power outage for several hours now. He listened to his father complain loudly that if the electricity was not restored soon, they would miss the football match between the Nigerian Super Eagles and the team from Zambia. He became absorbed with watching as the houseflies, which were probably commuting to and from the rubbish dump, stopped by to pay their respects to the pair on the balcony. They had been coming in groups of three or more, and the latest batch circled the glass that held his father's beer while the older man preoccupied himself with preventing them from diving into it. The sound of the gate opening and closing drew the little boy to the edge of the balcony, from where he saw Mama Sholanke, loaded with two bulging plastic shopping bags, come into the compound through the pedestrian gate. She called a greeting to Mallam as one of the gateman's friends let her in.

He dropped his toy on the floor and leaned over the balcony railing and said hello to Mama, who said hello right back and smiled warmly, asking him to say hello to his parents and sisters. He could hear the jingle of the keys echoing through the front door downstairs, and he looked over to his father, who was fanning himself with a newspaper.

Giving him a dirty look, his father scolded him impatiently, "You are too forward. Why can't you mind your own business? Who asked you to greet her now?"

He froze, facing the older man with his mouth wide open, about to utter a word in protest as the backs of his legs touched the cold iron bars of the balcony railing.

His father continued his scolding, not waiting for a response. "*Ehen!* She would not have seen you, but you had to open your big mouth; my friend, will you move away from that balcony and sit on this floor?" He pointed to the floor next to the chair he was seated on.

The little boy could see beads of sweat dotting his arms, his forehead, and the front of the white sleeveless vest he had on over a pair of shorts, which were also damp with sweat. He watched silently as his father picked up the glass in front of him and emptied the contents down his throat in what looked like one huge gulp. Standing up quickly, the older man threw his newspaper on the chair he had been

4

sitting on and went into the apartment. The boy remained quiet, as he was sure that his father would reappear with his leather belt in order to give him a good walloping for being so forward.

He heard the sound of the gate opening again; this time it was like a large crash. He peered downstairs, not daring to move closer to the railing, and noticed three strange-looking men engaged in a scuffle with Mallam and two of his friends. One of the men looked up, and from where he sat he could see that he was very dark-skinned, with a huge build, and his two front teeth, which were gold-plated, shone in the afternoon sun. His face was expressionless as he gave two quick nods to the man who stood next to him. Mallam and one of his friends were being shoved into the gatehouse by the third man while the two other men disappeared under the balcony. The little boy did not know what to make of the scene below him, and although he wanted to go in and tell his father what he saw, something told him that the older man might not be in the mood to hear any of his stories.

In a flash the huge dark-skinned man was standing next to him, pulling him up by his left armpit with one hand and pushing him into the living room. He had not even heard the front door open.

His heart beat faster as he searched for his father. The intruder said nothing but put his index finger on his lips, which was enough for him to stay quiet. As he sat quietly on the sofa, it took him a few seconds to see the gun in his right hand. He had seen guns on television, but it was the first time he had been in such close proximity to one.

At that moment he wondered what this strange man was doing in their home with a gun. He did not look like any of his father's friends; in fact he did not look familiar at all. A toothpick dangled from the intruder's lips, and from time to time he would pick his teeth to reveal the two gold teeth. The little boy watched him go back to the balcony and take the bottle of Star beer his father had left, take the toothpick out of his mouth, and put the bottle to his lips, instantly gulping down the contents. When he had satisfied himself, he threw the empty bottle next to the little boy on the sofa and simultaneously let out a loud, ugly belch, while putting the toothpick back in its original position. Staring at the bottle beside him, the boy strained his ears to hear the muffled tones coming from inside his parents' bedroom. The pleading voice he could make out sounded like his father's. Just then the door to the room opened, and another huge man came out and addressed the first man—who seemed to be his superior—as Ol' Boi. They spoke in rapid-fire Pidgin English before the second intruder reentered his parents' bedroom.

Ol' Boi gave him an amused look and asked him in perfect English, "What school do you go to?"

The little boy did not know why he lied, but it came out easily and almost immediately. He stuttered and gave Ol' Boi the name of a school he had heard of but never been to, and even before the intruder asked, he told him he was in Primary Five even though he was in Primary Three. Ol' Boi did not seem to notice or care about his lies, and his responses satisfied him. He remained standing motionless in the middle of the living room.

The next thing the little boy heard was a loud thud, followed by what sounded like his father moaning in pain. This was accompanied by a brusque, commanding voice. He sat there for what seemed to be an eternity. He felt like all the energy that he had in him had been completely drained. He could hear what sounded like pounding and banging of wood and rustling of clothes.

Ol' Boi hummed a tune that the little boy tried to make out but could not recognize. He did not ask his captive any more questions or seem to look in his direction, as he seemed to be satisfied that the boy did not plan on doing anything stupid. The little boy wished he had the courage to. His mind wandered to a number of different places, painting scenarios in which he could do something heroic to take control of the situation.

The return of Ol' Boi's companion jolted him back to reality. The second intruder held two bulging black plastic bags. Ol' Boi gestured that he should go with him. As they walked past the front door toward his parents' bedroom, he noticed the shadow of another figure through the door, which was slightly ajar. His parents' bedroom looked like a tornado had passed through it. The drawers of the dressing table, where his mother arranged her cosmetics, had been pulled out.

Doors of wardrobes were hanging open. Clothes, papers, and books littered the floor.

They walked quickly toward the bathroom suite connected to the room, and in the bathtub he saw his father seated with his hands tied in front of him and his mouth gagged with a thick piece of cloth. Tears spilled from his eyes as he noticed a huge bloody gash on the front of his father's head. His father looked at him, and the little boy could see relief in his eyes. Their companions asked him to get into the bathtub with his father, and he quickly obeyed, searching for standing room as his father's long frame had taken over the entire tub. The soles of his bare feet touched the cold, dry porcelain bathtub as a mixture of emotions raced through his body.

Their captors exited the bathroom, banging the door shut, and the little boy looked at his father, too frightened to say anything. The older man motioned to him with his eyes and a weak nod of his head to remain where he was. The blood from the gash on his father's head was running down his face, and it trickled past his left eye onto the cloth in his mouth, where it had begun to soak.

They remained in this position for what seemed like an eternity. His father was still bleeding in his bound and gagged state and the little boy was standing still, remembering the look in Ol' Boi's eyes.

The silence was deafening.

He looked away from his father, who lay still in the bathtub. He did not want to see any fear in the older man's eyes

Everything that happened next was so sudden, it was almost like a blur. He remembered feeling a wave of relief rushing over him as he saw his mother and his sisters and not being able to recognize the sound of his own voice as he cried like a baby.

There was the stampede of feet as some of Mallam's friends from downstairs rushed to untie his father and help the injured man out of the bathtub. Hours later he fell asleep with his head cradled in the crook of his mother's arm as he watched his baby sister looking at him curiously, her right thumb in her mouth as she sucked it furiously.

Some people would tell his father that he should be thankful because so-and-so was not so lucky and now his family was getting ready to bury him. In the kitchen the little boy would listen to his mother and the pastor's wife praying and thanking God. Later that day he would hear his mother telling one of his aunts that the intruders had made off with all of her gold trinkets, some of which she had not finished paying for yet. They learned that the robbers had had a car waiting outside, and they had also robbed Mama Sholanke downstairs. They never saw her again after the robbery. Traumatized by the incident, she left the apartment and moved in with one of her children, while members of her family later came to clear out what was left of her things. Within weeks the ground-floor apartment was vacant.

One of their earliest visitors after the incident was their elusive landlord, Alhaji Adisa, accompanied by his son, Uncle Sardine. Alhaji was not what the little boy had expected. He was a tall, skinny man with kind eyes, dressed simply in a *jalabiya,* with a white knitted cap on his head. He spoke in soft, reassuring tones and punctuated his sentences with "*Insha* Allah" and "*Alhamdu Lahi,*" and when he left he gave the children money, which their mother promptly collected from them and tucked in her purse.

The day after his visit, Uncle Sardine brought a welder to install an iron gate on the inside of the front door to the apartment, which they were told they could lock with a padlock. Even with that added security, they would not stay much longer in the apartment. The weekend after the incident they learned that four other houses in the area had been raided, and in one of them a man was shot and was in critical condition at the university teaching hospital. The children's mother was nervous and uneasy and nagged their father until he became frustrated. At night when the children were trying to sleep, they would hear their parents arguing in their bedroom.

Eventually their father found them another place to live, and their mother told them that they would have to go to a new school and make new friends. He still had his friend Bamidele's Voltron toy wrapped in a black plastic bag, hidden under a pile of clothes in his wardrobe. Bamidele had let him keep it after he had learned about the robbery; it was a very kind gesture especially since he knew that his friend was attached to the toy. Still, it would have been hard to explain this to his mother, so he kept the toy hidden.

Seated in the car early one evening as they drove home from visiting relatives, he was thinking of a tactical way to move it without his mother suspecting anything. The family was caught in slow-moving traffic, with their father behind the wheel and their mother in the front passenger seat while the little boy was in the back seat directly behind her. His two sisters were fast asleep next to him. He craned his neck to see what was going on and noticed that there was a checkpoint several cars ahead. The length of the street had been barricaded with two large planks on either side, and there was enough room left for one car to squeeze through following intense scrutiny of the vehicle's documents by a policeman. There must have been at least a dozen policemen at the checkpoint. On the side of the road close to him, there were some policemen attending to vehicles that had parked a few yards away, while other policemen were standing by idly. His eyes wandered to them. By this time it was their turn to be checked, and he could hear Daddy rolling down his window and speaking to the policeman in the respectful voice he reserved for older people.

The little boy was about to look away when he noticed something he had not expected to see. Standing about ten feet away from him, dressed in a police uniform and talking to another policeman, was Ol' Boi.

The little boy had not thought about him in the weeks since the incident. At first he thought his mind was playing tricks on him and it was just someone who looked like Ol' Boi, but at that moment the man he was speaking with said something that made Ol' Boi laugh, revealing two gold front teeth. The little boy gasped loudly and squinted to adjust his vision to make sure that there was no mistake. He confirmed that it was indeed Ol' Boi and he was indeed wearing a policeman's uniform. The intruder-turned-policeman did not see him, but the little boy saw him clearly. He glanced quickly at his father, who was facing the other side of the road, collecting the vehicle's paperwork from the policeman attending to him. Almost at the same time as he was about to draw his father's attention to Ol' Boi, the car accelerated forward, and he stared hard as he saw Ol' Boi's figure disappearing behind him. The little boy remained silent and motionless as he tried to understand what had just happened.

A Laughing Matter

Whenever we had a new washerman, my father-in-law would put two twenty-naira bills in the pocket of one of his pieces of clothing before handing them to me as part of the laundry.

It was bait.

According to him, if the washerman was honest, he would find the money and come back to the house and hand it back. If he was dishonest, he would wrongly assume that the money had been forgotten there and pocket it as his own.

Of course, if the latter happened, I was asked to let the washerman know that his services were no longer required. My father-in-law would then subject me to a thorough verbal analysis of the human character, preceded by a wordy lament of how he had just lost his hard-earned money because of my poor judgment. This was a speech that I found garrulous but that I had been subjected to on three different occasions. My reaction all three times was to try with everything I could muster to hide my true feelings and make an appearance that I was gaining some hitherto lacking knowledge. Each time, I vowed to myself that I would try to be a better judge of character—by, according to Papa, being able to read what a person can or can't do by their body language and the shiftiness, or lack thereof, of their eyes. Papa's approach was often belligerent and unpleasant, and no one should have had to endure such plain disrespect.

Today we were getting a new washerman. I had informed Papa about this the night before, and from what sounded like a mixture of a mumble and a grunt, I understood that he would have some clothes to add to the day's laundry. Still, it was too early in the morning to have to endure any churlish interactions with Papa, so I enlisted the help of Mercy, who knew him well enough not to be surprised by a frosty reception. My sister, Mercy and her friend Nneka had both been living with me for nearly a year, so they knew enough about Papa, but I chose Mercy because her threshold for tolerance was higher than Nneka's. Her mission was simply to cross the driveway that separated Papa's house from ours, collect a bag of clothes from Papa, and add it to the clothes for that week's laundry. I was busy making breakfast for the children when she returned—in less time than I had anticipated. I had my back to her and waited for some sign of the old man's mood that morning, which would be indicated to me in any message she would relay—*upset, furious,* and *irate* were among many adjectives on my list. When I did not hear anything, I glanced back at her. In response to the curious stare of my unasked question, she quickly explained that the bag of clothes had been waiting for her at the front door, and on seeing this she had picked them up and walked straight back to the house, not waiting for the old man to show up. The ultimate "Do Not Disturb" sign. I found this cat-and-mouse game that we played with Papa quite amusing, but sadly I had gotten used to this in the time we had lived here.

I had married a journalist, a writer and a poet. Ajibade, whom we all called Bade for short, was a simple man whose passion was writing. He came from a small family, just himself and his parents. I cherished his mother, who was soft-spoken, cordial, and respectful and not in the least bit overbearing, like some of the mothers-in-law I had heard about. His father, on the other hand, had always been hard to read. He never smiled and always gave me a suspicious look that, if I had something to hide, would have disarmed me completely. My own parents and siblings lived in another town—two days' journey away—and I hardly saw them at all.

I enjoyed my job as a primary school teacher, and my husband enjoyed his as a journalist writing for a local newspaper, sometimes having the opportunity to report on obscure facts. It was the best of times for some in the country and the worst of times for most.

Although the world described our beloved nation as one of the world's most successful oil producers, translating into one of the wealthiest nations on our side of the hemisphere, only a handful of the citizens enjoyed the benefits of this wealth.

Poverty glared you in the face everywhere you chose to look. Electricity supply was sporadic if at all. It seemed that every time you went to the market, the price of everything had tripled, leaving you to haggle over the price of a commodity with a hungry, haggard-looking old woman whose clothes hung on to her bony structure and whose eyes pleaded with you to be kind and generous. Everyone spewed out an endless litany of woes in reaction to the state of the nation. We all knew that we were suffering in the midst of plenty as a result of the selfish choices the ruling class was making, with little trickling down from above to the masses.

People often spoke of an uprising, a revolution, some sort of action that would serve as a catalyst for change. I had least expected it to come from so close to home.

Musings of a Subliminal Mind was the column that Bade wrote. With a witty and indirect approach, he deliberately targeted the excesses of the ruling elite, comparing their lifestyles to the reality that the average citizen had to contend with. The paper he wrote for had a moderate regional circulation, but his column was for the most part largely unnoticed.

Then the son of the minister of foreign affairs got married to the daughter of the minister of culture. The wedding ceremony took place in the United Kingdom, with a church service held in the same church where some members of the British royal family had been married a couple of months before. The Associated Press reported the story with estimates of the exorbitant cost of the wedding, making comparisons between the price tag and the ostentatiousness of the Nigerian wedding and the simple yet elegant British one. Typing away furiously on his worn-out typewriter by lantern light late into the night, Bade produced the article that would change our lives forever.

Perhaps it was the right time, but it was still amazing how the article became the reference point for the formation of the opposition movement that would become the bane of the ruling military government.

My husband, a self-described maverick, would make it clear that he did not belong to any side but was on the side of truth and justice, and his mission was to ensure that there was an equal spread of the national wealth rather than it being in the hands of a small, oppressive minority. I had always known him to be a tenacious advocate of civil rights, but nothing in my imagination prepared me for the turmoil that would come crashing through our lives. Within the space of the year, our small apartment became a beehive of activity as people came and went—some seeking advice, some seeking words of encouragement, some seeking some sort of indescribable redemption to lift them out of the quagmire that their lives consisted of.

In an unexpected twist of fate, his column achieved national fame, increasing the circulation of the paper from semiregional to national. He was given a double promotion. While all this was happening, we welcomed a son into the world, and perhaps it was in this new role of motherhood that I began to feel a sense of foreboding.

A lot was being said publicly about the military regime that had never been said before. Some reaction on their part would have given us a sense of where they stood in terms of the new direction that things were taking. But the higher-ups remained passive, almost like a silent time bomb waiting to go off.

Just before dawn on a Friday morning, that time bomb went off.

We were preparing to set out for the day when the door to the apartment was broken down and a dozen military policemen with loud, commanding voices invaded our space, shattering our lives and taking my husband with them. In record time my husband was bundled into a waiting unmarked vehicle while my voice grew hoarse and cracked as I howled and wailed in protest, ululations that alerted the whole neighborhood to the situation, our infant son cradled on my back all the time. My sister, Mercy, who had just moved in with us, looked on helplessly. There was nothing we could do.

Two male colleagues of my husband accompanied my mother-in law and me to the police headquarters to inquire about the reason for arrest. On arrival at the front desk, we were received by a haughty and overbearing female police officer who could not (would not) give us any information and advised us to seek legal counsel. Against my better judgment, I tried to plead to the female in her, citing my status as a wife and mother. Her face was devoid of any emotion as she announced that she had neither a husband nor a child, so she had no idea what I wanted her to do. With a mixture of degradation and despondency, we left the building and went in search of a lawyer.

It took us a whole month to find Bade. He had been taken to a prison in the north; it took another two months for us to be told what his crime was. Eight months after the ordeal began, he was released from prison with the charges dropped and a stern warning to keep his writing tasteful.

That warning fell on deaf ears. Something had been born in him when he was incarcerated. I like to believe that it was something that had been planted there for a long time and just needed the brief incarceration to germinate and begin to bear fruit. He would tell me that his pen was his sword and that being a plebeian himself, he was fighting for the cause of the common man. He was on an inexorable mission to ensure that the average citizen received a fair portion of the national cake by having some semblance of a decent life. It was his small way of drawing the attention of the world to the plight of the common man.

Our lives changed; he became more prolific in his writing but also sought after as a speaker in rallies with the tagline "Freedom, Equality, and Justice." His imprisonment had earned him a huge following, making him some sort of messiah, bringing the promise of redemption that the people yearned for.

I had to quit my job as a schoolteacher—the public school was funded by the government, and given the nature of my husband's activities, it was only a question of time before I would have been asked to leave. I located a small stall in one of the markets, where I started to sell children's books. My bookstore was in between a dry goods seller and a shoemaker. So the face of our family changed as did the nature of our livelihood. Husband: journalist turned political activist. Wife: teacher turned market woman.

Our lives were far from normal. We traded our cozy three-bedroom apartment in the suburbs for a one-bedroom shoebox in the middle of Lagos: the capital city. You could hear everything your neighbor did and said from within the confines of your home. Like the dutiful wife, I never complained; I took it in stride, praying for my family every day and hoping for a return to normalcy. I did not have a strong opinion like my husband when it came to such things. I was the product of a docile breed that just accepted things as they were, and if change came, I accepted it. If I was afraid of anything at all, it was that my child would grow up and osmotically adopt a similar approach to life as his father's. This was a fear that came to consume me even more when I discovered I was carrying our second child.

A group called Movement to Reduce the Suffering of the Masses (which adopted the uncanny acronym MOREMASS) declared my husband as their mentor. He attended a few of their rallies, citing the experiences of oppressed people who had overcome their situation by refusing to accept without action.

During this time the whole nation would experience an intense and debilitating fuel crisis, which would lead to a series of country-wide riots. To add insult to injury, while there was no petrol at home, several people were crossing the border to buy petrol from our Western neighbors. This further incensed people—our neighbors were a non-oil-producing nation who imported their petrol and petroleum products from us.

I hardly saw my husband during the weeks of the petroleum crisis, but there was no shortage of people in our home. Mercy was busy with her studies in fashion design school and tried the best she could when she was available. My mother-in-law and even the wives of fellow activists as well as colleagues were happy to come to our home to help me cook and clean and keep me company, especially as my belly began to balloon, announcing the pending arrival of a new child. Still, I was petrified. The military government's silence made us uneasy. Many wondered why there was no reaction to the demonstrations that were openly going on in every city in the country. Mobile policemen were often dispatched to monitor the riots, which were for the most part peaceful. There had only been one incident of attempted looting, which had been dealt with, and the MOREMASS leaders who were gaining more popularity were quick to inform the nation that any illegal activity was not endorsed by them and completely contrary to their mandate. Even though the government remained quiet, conversations with people indicated that something was brewing, and it would create a major catastrophe as far as the movement for equality was concerned. It seemed everywhere I turned there were whispers of a nameless fear.

There was an explosion in the administrative offices of the petroleum directorate. The unidentifiable charred remains of two men, who we were later told were employees of the petroleum directorate, were removed from the burnt building. The next sequence of events gave the nation an insight into how the Supreme Military Council worked. My husband was arrested at a rally. At a press conference held at the headquarters of the Supreme Military Council, two men were paraded before the general public. They declared that they were MOREMASS leaders and took responsibility for the explosion at the directorate. The members of MOREMASS were stupefied because neither the names nor the faces of these men were familiar to them. There was more to come. The men declared that their action had been instigated by my husband. The stench of foul play was pungent in the air as they went on to declare that they had a secret training ground and were planning a coup to overthrow the supreme military government and install my husband as the leader of the nation. It was a classic case of a setup. In record time a trial was held in a farcical kangaroo court. We would later learn that the judge's son was married to the supreme military ruler's niece. Such family ties did not bode well for us. I was not permitted to attend any of the proceedings because of my condition, but my mother-in-law attended every single one and even had the unpleasant experience of visiting her son in prison. She described him as gaunt and worn-out on the exterior, but he still carried inside that fearless spirit. He was the one who told her in hushed tones that the government had staged the explosion. Anyone with half a mind could easily have deduced that only the government was capable of having in their possession the heavy-duty explosives that were used to bring down the building. Many had already guessed that the charred remains that had been found in the building were taken from the public morgue—some of the many unclaimed bodies of victims of hit-and-runs that occurred with regularity in the city. They had been placed in the building before it was blown up. All this added to the list of crimes that my husband would be charged with—treason and murder the most heinous of all. He was sentenced to life imprisonment.

The allegations against the "MOREMASS leaders" were quickly dropped because of a plea deal—they had, after all, cooperated with the government and confessed to their crimes, and their reward was their freedom.

A month after the sentencing, my mother-in-law had a severe heart attack that left her in a coma for two days before she finally decided that it was not worth it and crossed over to the other side. Many said her heart had been broken and she could not bear to see her only son rot in prison while she was alive. Shortly after her death, I gave birth to a baby girl, and the same people were quick to say that my mother-in-law was back and obliged me to name my child after her. We named her Ayomide: *My Joy Has Arrived.*

Things had changed quickly following the sentencing, a lot of people of had thrown caution to the wind, and the crime rate had quadrupled. Fearing for my safety, friends and family asked that I relocate. My first instinct was to take the children to my parents' home, but my father was a staunch traditionalist and refused to have a daughter back whom he had handed over to another family in marriage.

However, Papa's residence consisted of two detached duplexes. He had always rented the second duplex out and was happy to rent it to us. When people expressed their horror that he would collect rent from his imprisoned son's family, he was quick to remind them that he was owed several years of pension by the government, and he wondered aloud how he was expected to survive if he allowed me and my children to stay in the house for free. So we moved to the house, on the outskirts of the city, and I found a job teaching in a private school a moderate distance from the house. I prepared to live a more or less obscure life raising my children as a single mother.

A sign of how the semicohabitation with Papa would go came the first day Mercy and I arrived with the children. It had been a long journey, which was made even longer because of an accident along the way. By the time we arrived at the house, it was late and we were exhausted and hungry and could not wait to get some much-needed rest. We were alarmed to find that the gates to the compound were locked from the inside. Papa had left a message with the next-door neighbor to let us know that he locked his gates after seven o'clock at night. It was the mortified neighbor who offered us a place to spend the night.

That was the first of many of Papa's idiosyncrasies we would have to endure. Shortly after we moved in, we would be joined in our household by Nneka, who was a friend of Mercy's and needed a place to stay. When we introduced her to Papa, his first words were "'I don't know why you need a housemaid...you and your sister are capable of looking after the house and the children yourselves." This after I had told him who Nneka was. The latter took the statement in stride by ignoring the older man. She and Mercy kept themselves busy with a new fashion business that they had started, and I noticed that Nneka always chose to carry on as if Papa did not exist. Who could blame her?

This morning I had been prepared for the worst, which could at the very best be a summoning in the form of a message delivered by Mercy. I was more than a little relieved when she brought his clothes to the house with no strings attached. I jumped into the day with a renewed vigor, happy to go through it without any acerbic remarks from a lonely geriatric. My commute to work consisted of two buses, and my only consolation was that we were all going to the same destination. Both of my children went to school with me. It was no small blessing that the school had a crèche attached to it, where my daughter could spend the day, and my son attended the Elementary school. There was never any question that Papa would allow us to use his car, and I preferred it because I was not ready to endure any disrespectful insults.

After waiting for longer than usual, we were on the second bus to our destination. Following a brief scuffle, my two children in tow, I managed to get a seat and balanced both children on my lap. There was a huge market two stops away from the stop for the school, and on most mornings like this, the bus was packed with market women jostling their wares for the day.

I had not paid much attention to a disheveled man who had boarded the bus at about the same time with us. He spoke slowly but articulately in clear tones, describing himself as an insurance loss adjuster in a previous life. According to him, things had started to go sour for him when his infant daughter got ill and was diagnosed with a terminal illness. His narration of how she was in a local hospital struggling for her life struck a chord with me, and my heart went out to him. It was not unusual to see grown men begging for assistance on the public buses. Many people responded positively to his request for contributions to help him to buy some much needed medication for his daughter. I cuddled my children a little closer and dug into my purse for some money, which I thought could make a difference. He was seated a couple of rows ahead of me, and when he turned to receive my contribution, I could not help but notice how familiar his face was. The bus was too crowded for me to interrogate him further, and as the bus pulled in to the next stop, he bade farewell to the passengers, thanking us for our contributions.

As he was about to descend from the bus, a well-dressed gentleman was trying to board. For some reason, which neither I nor the other passengers on the bus could understand, there was a brief altercation between him and this passenger. Words were exchanged before the driver, honking the horn, asked both men to either get on or get off.

The new passenger settled in his seat and the bus was on its way when one of the market women on the bus was bold enough to ask what the fracas was about. She rebuked the new passenger for failing to show more pity on a man struggling with family issues.

Letting out a guttural laugh, the new passenger swung around to the inquiring woman. "Which story did he tell you people on the bus this morning?" he asked. "Is it his mother or his daughter or even he himself that has some disease and is dying and needs help with medication? I hope nobody on this bus gave him any money, because if you did you can be sure to find him at the nearest beer parlor, using your money to feed his appetite for liquor."

The bus erupted into a cacophony of voices as many of the passengers expressed their outrage. One of the men on the bus volunteered to get down at the next stop and catch the bus in the opposite direction in order to go after him. Many people dismissed this as a futile attempt. It would be easy for the crook to deny whatever accusations were leveled against him. Many lamented the state of the nation as they wondered how someone who was so well-spoken and articulate could descend to such a level. I tried to wrap my mind around the fact that the gentleman who had narrated a heartbreaking story with such brilliant eloquence could actually be a con artist, who at this very moment could be using the money that he had dubiously extracted from well-meaning individuals to fuel some hopeless desire for alcohol. Yet why did he look so familiar? Where could I have seen him before?

I felt bile rise from my stomach as the bus approached our stop. It was as I prepared my little children to descend that my brain chose to unlock the compartment where this memory was stored. I froze for a millisecond but then placed my daughter securely on my back and firmly held my son's hand. I knew where I had seen the man's face before. In fact I had seen that face on the TV screen and in the papers for months. He had been one of the men who claimed to be one of the members of **MOREMASS**, who had alleged that my husband had instigated them to use to explosives to blow up the building of the petroleum directorate. I felt the blood in my body rush to my head. I even swooned a little bit but felt my son's grasp in my hand and my daughter squirm on my back. I took one step, then the other, and walked steadily toward the entrance to the school.

My early morning experience managed to dampen my whole day, and by the time we arrived at home that evening after an equally tiresome journey back, I felt like a dark cloud had been hovering over me the whole day. I was not prepared to deal with the message that Mercy tactfully delivered, indicating that Papa demanded my presence as soon as I returned. Handing over the children to her, I walked over to his residence.

I knocked on the front door twice. I listened for a response, and when I did not get one, I turned the knob and entered the house. Papa was seated at his usual position in a corner of the living room on one of the two chairs. It was his favorite chair—an armchair with faded patterned upholstery that must have been pretty when it was newer. He had his back to me, and I was not sure if he knew that I had come in. He was listening to the news coming out of the transistor radio on a table by his side—the signal was poor, so every now and then the announcer was interrupted by a crackle and a snap.

During one of those interruptions, I announced my presence with a greeting: "Good evening, sir."

The announcer was saying something about talks between the government and the university lecturers reaching a stalemate and that the university students who had already been home for six months would have to endure another period of waiting.

I was beginning to get irritated. I shifted my weight a little. This was classic Papa. I saw him raise his hand to scratch his head and decided it was another opportunity to repeat my greeting.

"Good eve—"

"Do you know how much a pensioner makes?" I was trying to find the right response when he continued. "In fact, what am I asking you that for?" Then to himself he said, "I think stupidity must be a disease, and I am catching it from her. How can I expect someone whose brain is always in reverse gear that makes them think backward to know the answer to a question like that?" He moved a little on his seat.

The announcer on the radio had moved to another piece of news, and I stood there wondering the best way to endure the humiliation I was about to face. He did not need to turn and look at me to tell me that the new washerman had made off with the money that he had put as bait, for me to know that this was the source of his acrimony.

I swallowed my saliva. It was not a lot, as my mouth was beginning to dry up. Here I was, the long-suffering wife. *Let it be over and done with,* I thought. *Tear me into as many pieces as you can imagine possible. There is hardly any part of me left anyway.*

He started to say something else when a voice I recognized as mine but still found hard to believe interrupted him: "*Ehen*, enough with the insults *jo*. In fact it stops today. What is it? So the washerman took your money, so what? Did anybody ask you to put money there? Maybe now you will learn your lesson. And for your information, that washerman is staying; I am not firing anybody. If you don't like it, you better start washing your clothes yourself." The voice paused to catch its breath. I was possessed by an irate woman with no respect for her elders. I was still trying to find a way to tame this demon that had taken over my senses when the voice continued: "Imagine the nonsense! After a long day at work. You did not even ask about your grandchildren. How they are doing? How our day was? All you care about is your stupid money. Whose brain is in reverse now? You better stop talking to me like that or you will continue to see this side of me, and I can guarantee you, I will not take it easy with you."

Papa remained silent for a few seconds. Then I heard him make a sound; it sounded like a grunt, but then I realized that it was a whimper, the prelude to what turned out to be an uncontrollable sobbing fit. It was the first time that I had seen this old man display any emotion other than hostility and anger. Even when his wife had died, he had not cried. I felt a rush of pity come over me.

The irate woman had left.

I was back!

I moved closer to him. He had his head in his hands as his body writhed with emotion. He was talking as he cried, but most of what he said was indiscernible. I could make out the words "My wife! My son!"

I knelt down next to him. I hesitated a little and then I started to speak: "Papa!" I said softly. "Don't cry!" How could someone so tough crumble to such a low level of vulnerability in seconds? Today was indeed a day created for surprises. I could not believe that I was trying to pacify him.

He looked up, and our faces were inches apart. His entire face was wet with tears. His eyes looked so sad. "I have been such a terrible old man," he said. I raised my hand to stop him from continuing, and surprisingly he kept quiet immediately. I took off my head tie and started to use it to wipe his face. He took it from me and continued to do so himself, breathing in and out. When he finished he sighed heavily. His face was now completely dry, and the only evidence of his sobbing fit was his raspy breathing.

There was an uneasy silence for several seconds, which I broke by saying, "Can you imagine that the university strike is still on?" I hoped that this would be enough to break the ice, and I sat down on the floor, not knowing what to expect.

Papa's hands shook a little, and then he said in a low voice, "My daughter, Imagine! This country is just getting worse!" We were starting over on a new page. It was the original stern Papa's voice that I was used to. Gone was the feeble, whimpering voice. It was almost as if I had imagined it, and he continued as he gestured for me to stand up from the floor and occupy the chair next to him. "There you have my son, languishing in jail for a crime that he clearly did not commit." His voice was getting a little bit more animated, the way it did when he talked about issues of the nation.

We talked for a long time, sometimes pausing to listen to the radio and commenting on what was said. When I left him, I knew things would never be the same again. We had shared something that night and showed each other sides of ourselves that neither of us knew existed. So I could become angry, and Papa could cry. It was almost as if we had swapped places. How many tears had I cried for my situation and how unfair life was?

As I walked past the clothesline and noticed the dry clothes moving with the evening breeze, I realized that neither Mercy nor Nneka had had a chance to take the clothes off the line, so I decided to do this myself. The first set of clothes I took were Papa's, and as I took the peg off them and proceeded to fold them, I noticed that stuck to the crease of the fold of one of the clothes were two twenty naira notes that had dried on. I guess the new washerman had found the carefully hidden money a little too late and proceeded to hang the notes to dry.

I threw my head back and laughed, letting my voice erupt into the evening sky. It had been a long time since I had laughed so loudly and so spontaneously, and I continued to do so as I took the rest of the clothes off the line.

Terra-Cotta Beauty

My mother died when I was four years old. I remember few things about her, but I do remember that in the mornings when she woke me up and carried me, she often smelled of the earth. It was the same matinal smell that my grandmother, who would end up raising me had. I found out the secret of that smell just before I turned twelve. She went to the back of the house, took the earth that was still damp with the fresh morning dew, put it on a banana leaf, and used it as face mask. The earth would sit on her face for all of ten minutes before she gently washed it away. By the time the ritual was over, her skin was left smooth, fresh, and supple. Long before the advent of expensive creams with glamorous names and age-defying promises, the women in my family had found the secret of their beauty in the richness of Mother Earth's soil.

Sadly, I did not continue this ritual when I grew up; perhaps it was that burden of guilt that led me to name my salon Terra-Cotta Beauty. It was a sort of homage to the women of my family and atonement for my guilt at not having continued the beauty tradition. Although who could really blame me? By the time I was at the age when I could independently continue the beauty ritual, the rich, loamy earth of my grandmother's backyard in the serene city of Ile-Ife had been replaced by the cold, hard concrete of the city of Yaba in the Lagos metropolis. I had moved to Lagos to begin to carve out a life of my own with Mister Fred Erhabor.

Fred's sister had moved next door to my grandmother around the time I turned eighteen. Widowed at an early age, she had turned to her only sibling and brother to play a patriarchal role in her family's life.

His frequent visits had led to a series of matchmaking meetings sneakily connived between my grandmother and Fred's sister, although I like to think that we played some part in falling in love with each other. Nevertheless, by the time he left to study for two years in the United Kingdom, Fred Erhabor had asked the demure and homely girl fifteen years his junior who lived next door to his sister for her hand in marriage, with a promise that they would be together as soon as he completed his studies.

There was a collective sigh of relief when he kept his promise, and we were married five years after we had first met. So Mabel Ogun became Mabel Erhabor. Content that he had sown his wild oats while he had been abroad, our families gave us their blessing as we moved to Lagos and settled down in a two-story house on the corner of Patey Street. Fred got a good job with the town planning commission and thus begun his years of dedicated work with the Nigerian Civil Service.

We had two children. Fred Junior was followed by his sister, Adesuwa. We had a peaceful and calm life; I kept the house neat and tidy while Fred went to work, and when they were old enough, the children began to carve out their own existences as they started school. Still, I always felt there was more to my life than being a wife and a mother. It was a feeling that nudged me silently at first but then began to roar a lot louder around the time Fred began to get bored with his work at the town planning commission and started to nurture thoughts of an early retirement. I had known that one of the pitfalls of marrying an older man was that at some point the task of looking after the family would fall on me. This was something that had been driven home by my grandmother, who by the time the events began to unfold had joined the rest of my ancestors in the land of the Great Beyond, which we all held a one-way ticket to.

I knew I needed to think of something to do that would keep our family afloat. Even though Fred was due a generous pension from the federal government, we had seen enough from successive military governments to know not to depend on this. I was already telling my husband that he needed to start a private practice to generate an income, a suggestion that fell on deaf ears. Fred had never been the business kind. True, I had my secretarial studies qualifications, but I had not used them in so long that they were not only redundant, but I could not keep in step with the rapidly changing new technology. I had to think of something, and fast. Fred Junior and Adesuwa would soon be starting their secondary school education. Time was waiting for no one, and my family was no exception.

The idea for Terra-Cotta Beauty came to me like an epiphany. I had always done Adesuwa's hair and received compliments for hers and mine. Fred's sister had visited and requested that I do her hair. When she reported back that she had received a ton of compliments from other women, including requests that I do their hair, I began to seriously contemplate converting the ground floor of the house into a salon.

"Think about it, Fred…" I said the night that I summed up the courage to bring it up. "Do we even need that much space?" When he remained silent but still listening, I continued, "We could save on rent and all that."

"You are forgetting one important thing," he said. "You don't have any formal training in hairdressing."

"Don't say that, Fred!" I tried to mask my indignation with a certain degree of forcefulness. "I have more training than any recent graduate from hairdressing school. Besides, no one needs to know that."

In a calmer tone, I continued, "It is a gamble, Fred. Just like every-thing in life…the only regret will be not trying."

"Very well, Mabel." He sounded defeated but slightly excited as he threw his hands up in the air.

So the wheels were set in motion. We used up most of our savings to do the construction that would convert the ground floor to a state-of-the-art salon; we bought the equipment we needed. I knew I would need to hire staff eventually, but for the time being, until I had an established roster of clients, I would do everything on my own. Not too few times, as I put the plans in place, I questioned my sanity. Who in their right mind opened a salon on more or less a whim? Whenever I summoned the courage to silence the voices of dissent, Fred's own voice, reminding me that I did not have any formal training in hair-dressing, would echo back to me, and I would silence that also.

The excitement in my children's faces kept me going. To them it was just one great big adventure. They did not need to know that I was calling on all the angels in heaven every day to see me through this crazy ride that I had put us through. Failure was not an option, and we just kept on going.

The night before the salon was set to open, I was the vision of anxiety. I had tried to calm my nerves by keeping busy, and there was no shortage of things to do, but still I entertained so many doubts that it was hard for me to fall asleep. Everything had been prepared just the way we had planned it. The salon was decorated, and all the equipment I needed was there. There were mirrors on all the opposite walls which was a nice effect as it made the room look more crowded than it really was. The children loved it and played with their images in the mirror. All was set; we had a sign outside, and we had sent flyers around the neighborhood informing everyone. My entire body was pumped with more adrenaline than I would have imagined possible. I tried to imagine how things would change for us now that everything we had been planning had finally fallen into place. More than any-thing, I was eager to see who would be the first person to walk into the salon to request for my services.

The next morning, with Fred gone to work and the children in school, I rearranged my single workstation for the umpteenth time, making sure that the combs and brushes had some kind of order in size so that I would look organized and professional when my first customer arrived. I examined myself in the mirror. Did I look like someone I would want to do my hair? I was able to see myself from all the angles courtesy of the mirrors on the wall. I adjusted my work apron, tucked my hair behind my ears. I put the kettle on and was day-dreaming about all the things that could possibly go wrong with this new venture I had so boldly started, when both the click of the kettle signifying the water had boiled and a single rap on the door jolted me back to life. At first I thought I had imagined the latter and waited for the second knock, this time not any louder than the first. I unlocked the door and plastered a smile on my face.

My first customer looked about my age, small in stature, with an unmistakable maternal aura, accentuated by her graying edges. She spoke softly, almost reluctantly, as if engaging in conversation was a chore she would rather not undertake. She wanted to have her hair pressed, and I started working on it with the determination to make a good first impression so that she would not only return but would also be an ambassador for my work and bring more people my way.

For the hour that I worked on her hair, she was mostly taciturn. She responded to my friendly questions with monosyllables and grimaces. My first offer for tea was graciously declined with a brisk no and a weak smile. I had prided myself on the fact that I was not only a good hairdresser but also a good conversation starter and a good listener, but all my efforts to engage my customer were stymied. I had wanted Terra-Cotta Beauty to be a place where women would be able to unwind, let loose, talk about themselves, find a common ground, a caring voice, a listening ear—elements of life they might not be able to find elsewhere. The chitchat and camaraderie were needed to put a spark in life. My first customer was so tightly wound that it seemed as if this was never going to happen. I did not even know her name. I had asked, but she had either not heard or pretended not to, and I did not pursue it further. The last thing I wanted to do was make her feel uncomfortable. The only voice we heard as I busied myself with her hair was the one coming out of the radio. By the time I was done with her hair and showed it to her in the mirror, I had given up any hope of seeing any spark. Her hair had been transformed into a mass of bouncy curls that brought out the shape of her face. I had done her hair and made her look beautiful, but deep inside I felt like a complete failure. It had all been so mechanical.

I was not prepared for what happened next. Her face was transformed yet again, this time with a smile a mile wide. I was still trying to recover from this when she asked in a soft voice if she could now have that tea that I had offered her. Our eyes met in the mirror in front of us as I nodded and hurried to fetch her some tea. As we sat down to drink tea together, I was able to tease out bits of her personal life while also telling her about me. That was how Mrs. Omotosho, whom we would know simply as Bade's mom, became my first customer at Terra-Cotta. Even when she moved from the neighborhood to the other side of the city, she would continue to come to my salon to get her hair done, and this for me was touching. She was not just a customer; she became a good friend.

With time more people would come and become frequent customers. The beauty salon hidden on the corner of Patey Street became quite popular. By the end of the first month, I had to hire additional help, and over the next few years, I was generating an income that was able to sustain our lives to the point that when Fred prepared for retirement, four years after I opened the salon, I was not only making enough money for us to live off but also had something to do every day.

One of the women in the wide array of characters coming to Terra-Cotta was Mrs. Jolayemi. She was one of those people who had experienced everything; whenever she was in the salon, there was never a dull moment. When one of our new moms complained that her baby was not sleeping through the night, Mrs. J, as we liked to call her, suggested that she put a drop of brandy in with the baby's last bottle for the night. We were all horrified by the advice, even more so when the next time she came to the salon, the young mother declared that not only had she tried it, but it had worked. Mrs. J was thus vindicated and from that moment on was looked on as the person to turn to for advice—even though she was glad to offer her advice, comments, or opinions even when they were not asked for.

As the salon grew, I started to employ people, some of whom stayed longer than others. Some of the girls who passed through the salon as my employees would eventually open salons of their own in other parts of the city. I bore no malice and was always thankful that Terra-Cotta Beauty had served as a stepping stone. I also knew that no matter how much I expanded, I did not want to leave the comfort of our home. That was the original plan, and besides, it was also the more convenient plan. I could wake up as early or as late as I wanted, although more often it was the former rather than the latter. Even when the children, now teenagers approaching university, were grown and able to prepare their breakfast for themselves on days that they needed to leave the house early, I still found a reason to wake up in the morning. My life evolved into some sort of pattern. I was often not sure how I did, but I made things happen any way I could. It was interesting the way things changed for us. The house lost its signature lemon-fresh scent and adopted a different scent which was a combination of coconut oil and heat-applied to hair. I would learn from my husband I smelled the same way. In spite of the not-so-subtle changes, I tried to make sure that I was on top of everything with Fred, my children, and my business. And I thought I was. But you know, sometimes life holds surprises that we are not prepared for, and the way we react to them can make a difference in the journey.

Sis Maureen, Fred's older sister developed a terminal illness and was in a hospital in Lagos. We had accepted that there was not much that the doctors could do for her, and it was just a question of time before she concluded her journey on earth. I went to visit her regularly, and it was during one of these visits that she revealed a hitherto well-kept secret. In a soft yet raspy voice, she began, "You remember one time Fred was posted temporarily to a place up-country?"

She was referring to a brief period when Fred had been temporarily stationed outside of Lagos. He had been gone for barely a year, standing in for a colleague, and it was close enough that he came home every weekend to be with me and the children. I had read somewhere that dying people often hallucinated and brought up memories from their past that would help them as they crossed over. Still, I was curious to know where she was going with this conversation and waited patiently as she took her time to continue. I realized that she was waiting for my not yet articulated response, so I acknowledged that I did remember.

She continued, "It turns out that he had a relationship with a lady over there who had a child for him. The lady came to see me a few years ago with the baby—a girl. After she left, I sent for Fred and confronted him. He did not deny it. He could not even if he wanted to; the child looks exactly like him. I told him to let you know so that maybe something good comes out of it."

My heart was pounding so hard, I thought my head was going to explode. I tried to digest the words. There was something about the way she emphasized the words "relationship" and "lady." There was something about the challenging way she said that last sentence. This was more than just malicious gossip designed to make me feel bad. This was motherly counsel. I tried to think of a dignified reaction to the news while at the same time come to terms with the realization that Fred had betrayed me. So this was what it felt like. At that moment I shook off any concern for myself. This must have been very difficult for my sister-in-law, and I looked at her. There were tears rolling down her face, which I delicately wiped away.

"I just thought you needed to hear this…I am sorry," she said.

I did not say anything. I wanted to thank her, but she did not seem like she needed any form of gratitude. It seemed more to me like she had given me a challenging task to accomplish, and it was now left to me to see if I was up to the task. I watched her as she took a long, deep breath and fell asleep. I like to think that she felt like a burden had been lifted off her shoulders.

It was not long after that that she passed away. Shortly after her funeral, armed with all the information I needed and without letting him know, I set out at the crack of dawn in search of Fred's daughter. I did not know what I would find when I got there. I did not know what sort of reception I would receive. I knew that my heart had been firmly tethered to Fred's, in what I had long thought was a mutual commitment of love. I had neither expected nor deserved a betrayal. But then again, nobody does.

When I returned home that evening, I was not alone. I came home with Fred's carbon copy. No one could dispute the fact that she was his child. He might as well have spat on the earth and molded her from the mixture. She had inherited a fair share of his features, right down to his distinct aquiline nose. When people questioned how I had been able to take a child from its mother, I would respond: "Because

I asked". It was that simple. When I met the mother of Fred's child, I could never find an explanation for what could have driven him into her arms. She was completely different from me in many ways. She also recognized that and, oddly enough, exhibited a certain degree of shame in acknowledging this. It was a simple recognition that Fred was never and could never be hers and by extension the child she had borne for him was better off with him than with her. In the twinkle of an eye and without much argument, I became the custodian of another child, a surrogate mother so to speak. I did not put much thought into it, and I would later realize that neither did the mother of Fred's child. For years, I would replay the brief conversation that we had, even though not many words were spoken. We spoke more with our eyes than we did with our mouths.

One thing I liked about Fred was that he showed his anger with the strongest form of reticence. He acknowledged the child but had no words for me. It must have been a shock to him: this bold form of impudence that I had found that gave me the temerity to bring evidence of his sexual infidelity into our home. He was the least of my concern, although to be honest I also questioned my action—I had taken a child away from her mother, albeit with little resistance, but time had taught me that no matter how well a child was cared for by another, insofar as the child's mother was still living, the child would ultimately seek its mother out. The time for that would come.

Fred Junior and Adesuwa accepted their younger sister with more love and fewer questions than I had expected. This made it a little harder for me to regret my decision. To be honest, I can't remember what her name was originally because I decided to rename her Enitanwa, which I thought suited her more. Fred did not put up any resistance to this decision, and we went back into the rhythm of our lives, almost as if this brief interlude had been nothing more than a short intermission in the middle of a theatrical play.

Of all the people who would work with me in the salon, Mama Yeside was perhaps the most unforgettable. She had shown up one morning when we were not so busy and immediately declared herself the greatest hair braider in the city. She went on a self-promotion monologue, stating that she could plait any hairstyle you could think of—*shuku, patewo, kolese* —and pointed to the plaits on her head. I put her to work immediately, and she lived up to her declaration. She would remain with me for years. She was not only hardworking but exceptionally honest too, thereby earning my unwavering trust, and would remain a constant in the salon for a long time.

By the time she arrived, Terra-Cotta Beauty had gained tremendous popularity as a place for people to enjoy getting their hair done. The salon always had upbeat high-life music blaring from the radio, the perfect soundtrack to accompany the smell of the products being used, and the smell of hair being straightened with the hot comb. Although we had customers coming in from near and far, the impact of the salon was more solidly felt by those who lived on and around Patey Street. While many came to get their hair done, some people came to enjoy the camaraderie, which there was no shortage of. For some reason it also became a central rallying point for all the happenings in the neighborhood. I did not encourage malicious gossip in the salon, even though many people (including myself) could often not resist it, but I tried to make sure that if a conversation was edging toward a direction that was not particularly favorable to a person, I would either change the topic or declare outright that it was not allowed in my establishment. It was really hard, especially when the topic was juicy. Sometimes you would have a customer begin to talk about how she had heard about such-and-such person's husband in the arms of another. This was a sore topic for me, having been betrayed myself and also because the woman in question happened to be one of my customers. I immediately veered the conversation to the state of the nation—a more appropriate issue for everyone as we were all struggling under the pressure.

One person who always seemed to have a strong opinion about the state of the nation was my first customer, Mrs. Omotosho. As I got to know her, I would learn that she was a woman of few words, but she immediately became vocal when it came time to talk about our ruling military government and how the masses were suffering in the midst of plenty. Our country had been blessed with a lot of oil wealth, but none of those blessings were felt by many of the people who needed it. The wealth was in the hands of very few. When Mrs. Omotosho was in the salon and started to speak about current issues, everyone remained silent and listened to her. Her son was a journalist, so we all knew that we were receiving authentic information. Mrs. Omotosho, in her mild-mannered way, condemned the excesses of our government. She pointed out the high expense of the recent wedding of the minister of culture's daughter and the son of the minister of foreign affairs. How civil servants could justify spending so much money was food for thought. Someone boldly asked if there was anything that we could do about it, and my friend was quick to add that her son was in the process of writing an exposé about it and we could not remain silent any longer. She said it so casually, and I was so proud of her. Little did we know that this exposé would catalyze a series of events. No one was prepared for the outcome. Bade Omotosho was a very credible journalist. Fred had been reading his column in our local paper for years, and I was proud of my claim to fame, when I had realized that his mother was my first customer in the salon. In his article he said things that many said in the corners of their home, beer parlors, and salons like mine but that many had not dared to mention in public. It not only catapulted him to fame, it also gave his little known newspaper much-needed popularity and somehow galvanized the once subdued people in the country to action. People started organizing peaceful protests.

The next time I saw Mrs. Omotosho, I could tell that she was more apprehensive than proud of the situation. She told me that she was glad that things were happening and perhaps the government would now pay attention to the things it needed to, but still, she secretly wished that someone else's family was wearing these shoes. We had put so little stock in the power of words that no one had expected Bade or his little read column to serve as the focal point for a revolution, which is what people were calling it. She had come to the salon that day with Mercy, her daughter-in-law's sister, who had become good friends with Adesuwa and Nneka, another young girl who lived in the neighborhood.

As we watched the girls chatter in one corner of the salon, she asked, "What future do these young ones have in a country like this?"

It was a loaded question, and my response was equally loaded as I parted her hair into sections. I sighed heavily and said, "The future is in the hands of the Almighty, who put us all on this earth for a reason, my sister. We can only do our best for these young people and hope and pray that this life will be good to them."

A few days after that conversation, Bade Omotosho was bundled out of his home in front of his wife, child, and sister-in-law, taken by military policemen to an unknown destination. It was a frightening incident, not just because no one knew where he was taken to, but also because there was no official obligation to let his family know where he was. Mrs. Omotosho was beside herself with worry and fear, and it began to weigh heavily on her. She came to the salon now not just to do her hair but more to seek our help. Fred had retired from civil service as a director of the institution he had worked in for years, and even though he was in his fifth year of retirement, he still knew some people in government who had some connections to the military government. But on that end we got nowhere. Fred was no longer relevant in the grand scheme of things; no one owed a pensioner any favors, even for the people he had helped to climb up the functionary ladder, it was too strong a price to pay. All we could do was wait.

I was infuriated.

I saw a mother worried beyond measure over the fate of her child and a young family that was slowly being torn apart. There was no shortage of people who offered advice. Some said the family should get a lawyer and sue the government; others said no one sued the government and won and they would be adding more to their woes if they tried that. I even heard some people cynically say that perhaps he had already been killed. It was a thought that I refused to entertain, and I held out hope. The interesting thing was that through all this, the resistance movement that had logically formed as a result of Bade's illuminating article grew stronger from the moment he was captured. Pockets of resistance movements were forming in every corner of the country. Even my son, Fred Junior, who by this time was about to start his second year in university, told of groups that had formed on his campus. Universities had long been the bedrock of some of the most successful political revolutions, and while neither his father nor I were surprised, I felt like the worst hypocrite when I cautioned Fred Junior against being a part of this. Thankfully my son was more inclined to be an engineer than a social activist.

It was around the time of Bade's arrest that the dogs in the neighborhood took to barking viciously at night. Everyone who came to the salon complained about how it was disrupting the nocturnal peace of their households. Usually when dogs started barking it heralded the arrival of robbers, but peace and tranquility had been the order for some time now, so it was a sort of mystery when the dogs started barking. We were thankful that no robbers showed up, but it did not make it less disruptive.

We had been questioning this for a couple of days when Mama Yeside came up with the explanation. In her characteristic matter-of-fact manner of speaking, she said that the spirit of a young child had been violently taken out of this world and was roaming the streets at night, confused about where it should go. This was why the dogs were barking; they could see this spirit at night. We listened with rapt attention as Mama Yeside advised that collective prayers were needed to appease this spirit and gently nudge it into the direction of its ethereal destination.

Later that day one of the women who came to get her hair done confirmed Mama Yeside's deduction by informing us that a young boy who had been walking down the street a couple of weeks before, had been run over by an out-of-control car. The child had died instantly before he could be taken to the hospital, and the mother was in a state of inconsolable grief. I was not particularly superstitious and at that time was borderline religious, but the one thing I knew was that if no one was doing anything to stop the violent barking at night, I was going to. I swung into action by organizing a three-day prayer meeting to be held at the salon after hours. Word of it spread throughout the neighborhood. Fred thought I was out of my mind, and we argued about it a bit.

"You are just going to expose yourself to all these charlatans who will begin to prophesy about this and that," he said indignantly when I announced that a prominent and well-known prophetess from one of the Celestial Churches was going to lead the prayers on the third day. He refused to be a part of it and recommended that the children also excuse themselves from the gathering of madness being organized by their mother. Fred Junior listened to his father and feigned some sort of illness the first night, and the last two nights he insisted that he had deadlines he needed to meet. While he stayed upstairs with his father, his sisters were with me all three nights.

Men, women, and children gathered in the salon each night. The salon was crowded to capacity as more and more people came in. The prayers went beyond our immediate need to send the itinerant spirit to its ultimate destination. There were prayers for people to be met at the points of their needs—job requests, knitting families back together, praying for children to do well in school; it was a steady stream of prayers. I knew a lot of people were hurting, especially when the morning after the first night of prayers, my employees noticed little things missing in the salon: combs and small hand dryers had been cleverly pilfered.

On the second night we were more vigilant about locking things up and placing certain people at strategic points of the salon to deter even the boldest of petty criminals. I saw people each night that I hardly saw—even the elusive Mrs. Uchendu, who many said was a devout Catholic and would not be seen in a Pentecostal church, joined us on one of those nights. Mrs. Kalu, who held some high position in a commercial bank and whom many described as arrogant, showed herself to be a prayer warrior as she brought the house down with a long and powerful prayer. Perception is always different from reality.

All three nights were pretty rowdy, especially when the time came for prayers, preceded by singing and clapping. I watched the faces of those gathered, which contorted in expressions of agony as they laid their petitions before their Creator.

On the third night, the prophetess graced us with her holy presence. Someone announced that the mother of the deceased child was present, and we watched as a gaunt, weathered-down figure made its way to the center of the room and knelt down before the prophetess as special prayers were said for her. A pall fell over the gathering, and then it was all over. I went away thinking that we were all expectant for something that was beyond hoping that the neighborhood dogs stopped barking at night, and they did stop. What surprised me more were the people who would come to the salon or stop me in the street and tell me how their lives had been transformed since those three nights of prayer. I realized that even though our prayers had sent an itinerant young spirit to its heavenly destination, what I had done more on a whim than anything else had had some unintended consequences. I went from being borderline religious to being more fervent in my spiritual life.

Shortly after the prayer sessions, we received news that Bade Omotosho was languishing in a jail cell somewhere in the northern part of the country. The news was confirmed by his journalist colleagues. The challenge remaining was what we could do to set him free. No one we knew had the clout or connections such a task required. Crestfallen, we realized that the best and maybe the safest course of action was to wait it out and hope for the best. The Omotoshos needed our support now more than ever before. Mr. Omotosho, whom everyone called Papa, remained a bit of an enigma, not just to me but to Fred. We would visit them in their home, and he seemed so distant, even nonchalant about the way the situation had affected the entire family. He seemed to act as if he could not notice that his wife was shrinking and aging. He carried on as if nothing was wrong. As I got to know them, I realized that it might have all been a front. Perhaps underneath that somewhat harsh exterior was a human soul that was also aching, and the only way it knew how to address the situation was to act churlish.

Then one day, without any prior notice, it all ended. Bade Omotosho walked into his parents' home—gaunt and frail. His mother held on to his skeletal frame like it was the most precious element in her world. All of us gave a collective sigh of relief, thankful that things were now back to normal.

Fred Junior graduated from university with stratospheric grades and job offers lined up. His father and I were so proud of him. Adesuwa had not done so well in the university entrance exams and was now taking remedial classes. Enitanwa was now in her first year in secondary school. A voracious reader, she told anyone who would care to listen (and many did) that she was going to be a lawyer. Observing the way she argued with her older siblings and most often got her way after brilliantly stating her case, I did not doubt it myself.

The salon was doing well. We had crossed the ten year mark and shortly before that we had broken even and were on a constant profit-making wave. No matter how bad things were in the country, women still wanted to look good and fix their hair. I was always busy trying to find a way to make the salon more innovative, a cut above the others, to give my customers a reason to come to us and not one of the many others that had started to spring up nearby.

Our calm and serene neighborhood was also changing. Literally overnight a series of thefts began to occur in the houses around us. They were primarily petty thefts, but we were all astounded by their audacity. A family having lunch one Saturday afternoon had left their front door unlocked. Two young men had walked in with guns, demanded money and other material possessions, and walked out with them. It was almost like a social visit as they even demanded to be fed before they left. Thankfully no one was harmed. But this was not always the case, and stories circulated of people who had lost their lives just because they put up the slightest bit of resistance. Everyone blamed the state of the nation, and more people were speaking out against the government; they demanded an elected one, a government for the people, by the people. The usual refrain was that things would be better if the military stayed in the barracks where they belonged and the civilians took care of the political side of things. More as a form of tokenism than anything else, the military government announced that it was going to allow district elections, thereby opening the door to the much-demanded democracy. We could now choose our local government representatives. Almost overnight, posters of smiling faces were plastered all over the neighborhood. Customers would

42

come in campaigning for this or that person. Neither Fred nor I were interested in politics, but we were surprised by the number of people who were. Some of our neighbors who we had not realized were politically inclined were suddenly vocal politicians, campaigning on every street corner. Although to my customers and the rest of the world, I portrayed ambivalence and disinterest, deep inside I was very excited. This was the start of a new era. We could actually get to select someone who would lead us at the grassroots, and once that was done, the sky was the limit. Pretty soon we would be voting for our very own president, just like elsewhere in the civilized world.

After months of campaigning, the day arrived when we could cast our votes. Much to my disappointment, neither Fred nor I, nor anyone in our polling center, could cast a single ballot. When we arrived in the morning to vote at our registered center, we were informed that the ballot boxes had not arrived. After waiting for close to an hour, we decided it would be safer to wait at home and come back in the afternoon. By the afternoon, throngs of people were waiting at the polling center. Frazzled election officials kept on trying to reassure the angry voters that all would soon be resolved. We waited another hour, and nothing happened. I went home while Fred stayed, chatting with our neighbors. I was bored and irritated. Even more, the salon was closed because all businesses had been ordered to remain closed for elections, which were clearly not taking place. By nightfall no one had cast a single ballot. Radio stations had already started announcing that ballots were being counted in certain districts. Election Day would be ending with no one voting in our neighborhood. This made for a lot of unhappy people.

The ballot boxes never showed up. The spokesperson for the electoral council, who had spent most of the day reassuring us, left with a black eye and a missing front tooth. Fred returned home describing the worst sort of chaos he had ever seen. In the end a group of military policemen had shown up and shot in the air, and the crowd was dispersed.

When the winners of the local government elections were announced, we were all very surprised. Winners in certain districts had never even been on the ballot. It turned out that the experience in our neighborhood was almost the same everywhere around the country. A handful of people claimed that they had voted and went on the national news to share their experience. No one believed them. We all felt that we had been duped by a government that wanted to remain in power and continue to deceive the people. The elections had only worsened the situation in the country.

Shortly after this, Fred Junior began to show up at the house with a young girl whom he introduced to us as Labake. I gathered that she had been partially educated in Britain and came from a rather wealthy family. This probably explained why she had an aura of superiority. While part of me was impressed that Fred Junior could successfully woo a girl of that caliber, I was also a bit concerned by her pompous attitude. One afternoon during a particularly busy period at the salon, she and Fred Junior came to see us. After we exchanged pleasantries, my son went up to speak with his father, while she, perhaps to give them some privacy, remained in the waiting area of the salon. I could tell that all eyes were on her, especially since it was very rare for Fred Junior to come home with a lady friend.

As I worked on a client's hair, I asked her again (for the third time) if she would like something to eat or drink. She replied with a plastic smile and a sharp "No, thank you!" I continued, "You know, you are welcome any time to come over to the salon to do your hair." She did not look up as she rummaged through her handbag, searching for something. "Thank you, ma, but I don't let just anybody touch my hair."

A creepy silence fell over the salon. Everyone stopped chattering and looked in her direction. I did not look up, but I knew that the searing looks she was receiving could have shredded her into a million pieces. For a few seconds, I was completely immobile, and then I continued working on my client's hair because I knew the people looking at her were also looking at me, expecting a reaction. I was determined to keep my composure. It was such an unnecessary remark but said so casually, without the slightest hint of malice. I knew right away that not only did she mean every word of it, she also did not realize what she had just said—a clear indication of poor breeding. This was a child who had been born into wealth and had probably received all the best that money had to offer, but someone had left out some of the more important elements of life, which included a polite consideration of the feelings of others. Part of me was slightly annoyed that my son would choose to associate himself with someone like this, let alone make her the special person in his life. Most of me felt a maternal obligation to correct her and set her straight. But no, not now. And certainly not in front of all these people who were given her withering gazes and waiting for the perfect opportunity to swoop down on her and tear her apart, piece by haughty piece. I remained silent not for her sake but mostly for Fred Junior's. It would not serve them well if Labake were humiliated in front of all these people.

Fred Junior came down shortly after, gave me the customary kiss on the cheek, and bade everyone farewell. The salon resumed its original rhythm that had been interrupted following Labake's declaration. As I watched them leave, I saw my son put his hand possessively around Labake's waist, and it was at that moment that I knew he was going to marry her.

They announced their engagement less than a year later, and Fred and I went to visit Labake's parents as we prepared for the wedding. Folarin Lawson was from old Lagos money. His great-grandfather had made so much money back in the day that it was enough for the future generations to live on and not raise a finger, or so I was told. That did not stop them from achieving their own accomplishments, and Labake's father had trained as an engineer before setting up his own company, where Fred Junior worked. He had met Labake when her father had invited him over to dinner one night—an invitation that had "*matchmaker*" written all over it, and the rest was history.

There were three other children, whose given names all started with the letter L: Lanre, Lawunmi, and (the only boy) Lakunle. The hairdresser in me could not help noticing that Labake's mom had the worst kind of *jheri* curls that I had ever seen, and this was my first impression of her. Her hair was too greasy, and the curls were static. I suspected that she did not let just anyone touch her hair, but unlike her daughter, whose hair was pretty decent, Ronke Lawson's hair was just awful. I mentioned this to Fred when we got home that evening, and he chastised me for always criticizing other people's hair if I was not the one who worked on it. My verdict was simple: money did not buy elegance.

The date for the wedding was set; it all seemed surreal to me. I would have preferred for the wedding to be simple and elegant, but it was the bride's day, and she and her family had other ideas. So Fred Junior had a society wedding, and we even got to have our photo in the national paper.

Much to my surprise, shortly after they were married and had settled down in their own place, Fred Junior would come to visit us with increasing regularity, on an almost daily basis. It was an unusual detour from his commute home, and at first I did not comment or question his visits—I was always happy to see my son. But it became a source of growing concern for me, more so when it seemed that the reason for his visits was always centered on a need to be fed. He would ask for this almost immediately he arrived. Enitanwa, who was now old enough to wield her mettle in the kitchen and took charge of most of the culinary needs of the household, was the one who first alerted me to this as she jokingly described how Fred Junior was always ready to devour anything that was placed before him and once done, he would express his satisfaction with a loud belch that was common among those who had been deprived of nourishment. However, she was not laughing when a few weeks later she confided in me that Fred Junior had now resorted to placing orders to take home. She did this half complaining: "How am I supposed to make good grades if I am cooking for two Erhabor households?" And half scandalmongering: "If you ask me, something is wrong somewhere!"

I was also convinced that something was amiss. It was quite unusual for a recently married man to rely on his mother and sisters for his culinary delights, unless of course his wife did not know how to cook. You did not need to be a clairvoyant to make this deduction. I resolved to get to the bottom of this, but it would be hard, since I knew that Fred Junior would probably defend his wife with every bone in his body, and Labake and I still did not have the sort of mother-daughter relationship that I longed for. She was often standoffish and aloof in her association with me, and a confrontation would only worsen things. I needed to give it time, and this was what I did until Labake came to me.

It was a Saturday morning, and the two Freds had taken to playing golf on those days. When Fred Junior came to pick his father up, his wife accompanied him. I knew it must have been difficult for her to come to me, and she approached me as meekly as she could. She confessed to me that her expertise in the kitchen did not extend beyond the preparation of crisply fried plantain and a light omelet. She had noticed that Fred was always eating certain delicacies that she did not know how to prepare and would be willing to learn. This act of humility was not only touching but also a testament of the sort of love that she had for my son. I was moved beyond words and wholeheartedly agreed to tutor her to the best of my ability. Labake did not become a great cook overnight. It took a lot of work. At first Fred Senior offered to stand as a guinea pig to these culinary experiments, but this offer was quickly relinquished at the second failed attempt at making vegetable stew. I knew that we had a lot of work on our hands. Labake did not accept her shortcomings with any form of defeat; each failure strengthened her resolve to get it right the next time. My girls, who had been cooking since they were old enough to do so, were awestruck by a grown woman who could not cook. When they expressed this with uncontrollable laughter, I was quick to tell them off for thinking that everyone had the same sort of upbringing that they had had.

The one thing I enjoyed about the cooking lessons was that it gave me a chance to get to know Labake better. With time her icy disposition began to thaw, and I could see that she had held this barrier up more out of fear than anything else. Perhaps she was scared that she would not be accepted. It was then that I was able to observe and appreciate some of the qualities that must have made Fred Junior fall in love with her in the first place. Since her visits meant that she would inevitably end up in the salon, she finally let her guard down and allowed "just anybody" to do her hair. All was forgotten and forgiven, especially when she cooked a splendid meal for the family that we all enjoyed.

The fact that Labake was once cold and frosty and could not cook, was an episode that resided in the distant past, never to be revisited.

Then Bade Omotosho was arrested again. Since his first arrest, he had become a vociferous critic of a government that had not changed in spite of more and more groups rising up against it. Bade was oblivious to the trauma that he was putting his family through. His mother was back to doing her hair at the salon, and these days we spent more time talking about him than actually doing hair.

The second arrest was clearly more calculated than the first. He was speaking at a rally and was picked up in full view of the public. His column, coupled with his previous arrest, had catapulted him to a fame he neither cherished nor desired. It also meant that his had become a household name. We heard about it on the radio in the salon during our busy period. There was a moment of silence, followed by a loud, raucous disorder. Everyone had an opinion. I was worried about his mother, his wife (who at this time was expecting their second child) and their little son. My heart was filled with a rage I could not describe. Part of it was directed at Bade, who had been advised to live a quiet life away from the public glare, and part of it was for a government that felt it could do anything it wanted just because it could. There was no justice in this world.

We did not see the Omotosho family for weeks. Since she knew where her son was this time, Mrs. Omotosho visited him in his jail cell in the prison in the central part of the city. She refused to let anyone accompany her. Her husband showed no interest in doing so, but when I insisted, it became a little bit of an argument, so I let it go. I got updates from Mercy, who said that Bade's mom would rise at the crack of dawn with the meals that she prepared for her son and report to his jail cell as early as she could. Some days she was allowed to feed him; other days she would return home with the food. The few times I saw her and tried to talk to her, my advice fell on deaf ears. It was Mercy who was caught in the middle of the furor, and I felt sorry for her. She was the go-between Bade's mom and her sister—his wife. The second arrest had more or less torn them apart. The younger woman blamed her mother-in-law for encouraging her son to continue with his activism even though he had a young family to look after. It was a baseless accusation, but sometimes, when people are faced with circumstances they cannot control, they have to blame someone, and the person closest to them is often the victim.

I had a chat with Lilian, Bade's wife, and got her to see reason, that there was no point in putting the blame for anything on anyone's doorstep. I was glad when things were patched up between the two women, more so that it happened just when the government leveled its charges against Bade, accusing him of execrable crimes that everyone knew he was innocent of. The two women needed each other now more than ever before. We all knew that Bade would be languishing in jail for a long time, at least until this government left power.

We all had our personal struggles, and it was hard to see the family going through this period. It was easier for everyone to go back to their routine. My life was very busy, and even though I longed to do more to help, I realized that there was less I could do than I would have liked. I had not realized that fate had a special plan just waiting around the corner for me.

It was Mama Yeside who first alerted me to the fact that something was going on with Adesuwa. She was still taking remedial classes for the university entrance exams. Unlike Fred Junior and Enitanwa, who would study without being asked, Adesuwa needed to be pushed extra hard. So when Mama Yeside told me that she had found her at the back of the house throwing up, I immediately assumed that I had pushed my child too hard and she was now ill. The doubtful look on Mama Yeside's face would continue to haunt me for months. She did not need to say anything.

That evening after dinner, I pulled Adesuwa into the living room and pointedly asked her, "Is there anything you need to tell me?" Fred was sitting in a corner, getting ready to read the newspaper. When I had shared my suspicions with him earlier, he had told me that I was jumping to conclusions unnecessarily: "Mabel, not every female who throws up is pregnant." But mother's instinct told me that this was what it was. The silence that followed my question almost confirmed it. My daughter looked down and did not look up for what seemed like an eternity. When she did, her eyes were filled with tears. She still did not say anything and just nodded weakly. I tried to take in the unspoken words.

Speechless, I turned to Fred for some semblance of a reaction. He had set the newspaper aside and was now staring into space. It was the first time I had turned to him for strength. I was too weak for words, and Fred's passive reaction built up an anger in me that I struggled to suppress the best way that I could, by keeping quiet. A million thoughts went through my head. I was still waiting for a reaction from Fred, and the silence hung heavily in the room. I felt like screaming, "What is wrong with you?" at Fred. Any other father would have been yelling fire and brimstone, calling for the head of the person who dared to defile his daughter, demanding his head on a platter. Instead Fred just sat there, looking morose. I tried to decipher the unspoken words. But what does one even say at a time like this? I felt so empty. I could see Adesuwa from the corner of my eye, but I was too sick with fear, disappointment, shame, and annoyance to even look at her, let alone say anything. I walked past her, not knowing where I was going or what I was going to do. I took the stairs down to the salon. I heard Fred tell Adesuwa to go to her room and we would continue the conversation in the morning.

The silence of the salon embraced me, and although I longed for Fred to come down to join me and give me some reassuring words, I knew that that was not his style, and he was willing to give me my space. I tried to wrap my head around how this could have happened without me knowing. I longed to transport myself to an alternate universe where this was happening to someone else and not me. That was what I was good at. I could provide the help and support needed to someone else whose daughter was going through something like this. Faced with it myself, I felt the strongest form of helplessness that I had ever felt. I don't know how long I had been down there, enjoying the misery of my company, battling a myriad of "what if" thoughts, when I heard a knock on the door. At first I thought I had imagined it, but after several seconds, it came again. We rarely had visitors after hours on the weekdays in the salon, and I wondered who it could be.

I looked through the window and saw Nneka Uchendu. I feared the worst and asked her if everything was okay at home. As she tried to respond, she burst into tears. It was an eruption that had clearly been building up for a while, and I let her continue while I got her a glass of water. Between sobs, she explained that she had been accused of stealing from a neighbor's house, and she had not been given a chance to explain that she was merely returning what had been stolen by someone else. Her father had asked her to leave the house, and she had nowhere else to go. Her story sounded odd, and while I deliberated the facts and tried to understand, I could not help but question her father's actions. I was of the school of thought that the greater the crime the child committed, the greater the desire of the child to be loved. I thought about my own daughter, who had made an announcement that every parent wanted to hear, but certainly only when the time was right. I could not imagine asking Adesuwa to leave her home tonight. There was never any value in treating your child like a common criminal.

I had known Nneka for a long time now, albeit from afar. I knew less about her family than I did about many of the families that lived in the streets that adjoined ours. She struck me as a shy and polite child. Even though she and Adesuwa were good friends, I was not particularly close to her parents, whom I considered cordial and not overly friendly. They liked to keep to themselves, and some in the neighborhood considered them a bit odd. But they were gracious enough to send us a Christmas card every year, something we reciprocated according to Fred's policy of only sending cards to those who sent them to us, lest we spend a fortune sending cards to people who did not need them. I understood from the people who talked about these things that Nneka did well in school. There was some talk that her father had been disappointed because he had wanted her to study medicine and she was studying something else. My mind was cluttered with many thoughts. I tried to rummage through to find the appropriate story I had heard about Nneka, but for now I knew there was no doubt in my mind that Nneka would have to spend the night here. It was too late, in my opinion, to accompany her home, and whatever her crime, I suspected it was too sore and fresh in her parents' minds for them to want to entertain any visitors, even if their purpose was to intervene, and least of all people that they barely knew. I was glad that Nneka had had the presence of mind to come to our house. I could not begin to imagine where she could have ended up at that time of the night.

I sent Nneka up to Adesuwa's room, knowing that the two of them would spend the rest of the night sharing secrets and telling each other what they had been up to. First thing in the morning, as early as possible, Fred and I would call on the Uchendus. I knew Benedict Uchendu left rather early in the morning and it would be best to catch him before he left.

Fred was still awake when I entered our bedroom. I knew he was waiting for me to start the conversation, but what I told him was not what he had expected. I explained the situation to him and that we would have to go and see the Uchendus first thing in the morning. We did not raise the Adesuwa issue, and for some reason I was somewhat relieved by the brouhaha in the Uchendu household. Perhaps it was a God-given gift to give me more time to digest our current dilemma and have the proper reaction and solution to it. I fell asleep wondering what state of mind Mrs. Uchendu would be in, knowing that her child had been evicted from their home and left to fend for herself in the outside world.

I got a chance to see for myself when she let us in the next morning. She looked like she had not slept a wink the night before. A wave of relief filled her face as I informed her that her older daughter was at our place and had spent the night there. She seemed to relax but was not altogether calm. When Mr. Uchendu appeared, I let Fred do the talking as I tried to interpret the situation. It was clear from the moment he appeared that any form of mediation was neither welcome nor needed. The fact that we were not invited to sit down gave me a sense that our mission would not be successful. For some reason that I could not understand, Mr. Uchendu had made up his mind, and he did not seem to want to waver from it. I caught snatches of what Fred was saying as I read between the lines. Mrs. Uchendu was clearly beholden to her husband. Their younger daughter, who hastily walked past us and into the kitchen, also seemed fearful of her father. On any other day I would have shown my irritation, but my teenage daughter had just announced that she was with child, amd that weighed heavily on my mind. As we hurried to leave, I turned and took one last look at Mrs. Uchendu. Our eyes met, and in those eyes I saw a deep sadness. At that moment I did not care what her daughter may have done; I felt sorry for a mother who was missing a chance to love on her daughter. I was thankful for my child, who I knew was nursing a great deal of remorse and regret, knowing that her parents were probably disappointed in her.

As we walked back to the house, Fred took my hand and squeezed it tightly. It was a gesture that carried with it the reassurance that all would be well.

I spoke first. "Imagine if she had not come to us and had decided to do something on her own."

Fred sighed heavily and spoke calmly. "Let's be thankful that she did not do something on her own…no good would have come out of it." He paused. "It is not the best situation that she should be in, but at least she is here, and we should do what we can to help her. It's the least we can do, which is more than I can say for the jokers we are coming from." He gestured his head in their direction.

"You handled that well, dear," I whispered. "I wonder what they expected her to do…I hope he comes back to his senses soon. Their daughter needs them, no matter what her crime is."

"Well, we will just have to do the best we can to help them both."

The salon would be opening soon, and I mentally prepared myself for this as we entered the house. The smell of fried eggs filled the air as we got upstairs. Fred took Enitanwa to school, and as I prepared to start my day, I watched the two teenage girls silently working in my kitchen. I looked at my daughter and tried to picture a little one nestled in a corner of her womb in the embryonic stages of development. I had no more resentment or regret. It was exciting to think that Fred and I were going to be grandparents, earlier than we expected, but this was God's way of starting the new generation of our family. All the same we needed to have a talk with Adesuwa and

53

try to resolve certain issues. I would soon realize that the tsunami of events that was passing through this season had yet another wave to make before it left

When Mercy came into the salon just as we opened up for business that morning and I saw the defeated look on her face, I instantly interpreted it to mean that something had happened to Bade. I was certainly not prepared to learn that Mrs. Omotosho had suffered a massive heart attack and was lying in the hospital in a comatose state. I sank into one of the salon's chairs, weak at the knees, my mind reeling. Mercy's final words struck a deep blow: they were not sure that she would make it.

I cast my mind back to the last time I had seen her. She had looked so weak and broken. I had known that nothing I would have said could have eased her pain; instead I had extracted a promise from Mercy to keep a closer eye on her. It was Mercy who had found her, and I could read guilt in her eyes, as if she felt she could have done more. What could anyone have done?

The doctors were right in their prediction. Two days after she went into the coma, my friend decided there was nothing more left for her to do and crossed over to the other side. For an extraordinary person, Bade's mom had an ordinary funeral. Her son was not allowed to attend, which made all of us despair even more. There were so many things that we had no control over. It took me a while to understand that she was really gone. It was almost like a sick joke. Just like a whiff of smoke, she had come into our lives, and the next thing she had disappeared into evanescence. How did one explain that? My mind would always go back to the first time she had come to Terra-Cotta Beauty—my first customer, timid and quiet, mild-mannered and unassuming. She had come in with no airs or graces. Everyone who knew her had something good to say about her.

My life was in a total state of confusion. I missed my friend and mourned her and the tragic set of circumstances that had led to her demise. I had never felt so directionless. Yet I knew I had to get moving in order to keep things going. There was Bade's wife, Lilian, who was heavy with child and prepared to bring her child into this world in the midst of all this tribulation. We had to remain strong for her. And then there was Adesuwa. In spite of it all, there was no one more confused than a pregnant teenager. I had allowed my disappointment to get the better of me. I needed to be there for my daughter. Life did not have a rewind button, and now was the time to press play and keep moving on.

So we finally had our tearful chat. I kept Fred out of it while I asked her some pointed questions. I think Bade's mom's passing and the suddenness of it had made me come to terms with certain realities. No one ever wished for their unmarried teenage daughter to become pregnant. Yet things could still be worse. I resolved to look at the bright side of things. We were preparing to welcome a new life in our family, heralding a new generation. Fred and I were going to be grandparents. Yet, there were certain practicalities that needed to be sorted out.

The father's name was Afolabi Durosimi, and they had met at the remedial school she was attending. They were in love and had only tried it once. Once had been enough to get her pregnant. It was somewhat consoling to learn that it had never occurred to them to get rid of the pregnancy. It had been several weeks since Adesuwa had seen him, and I was getting worried. I think one of the first mistakes that I made was to take matters into my own hands. I decided that it was wise to seek out Afolabi's mother and try to see how we could combine our maternal prowess to make the outcome successful. I think I may have taken it for granted that all women were the same. I was so naïve.

It was not hard to find out where the Durosimis lived. It was not hard to find out his mother's schedule. I was not sure if her son had told her about my daughter and decided to play it calmly. I did not realize what was in store for me. It was one of the most unpleasant experiences of my life. Mrs. Durosimi knew about that "Erhabor girl." She belligerently told me that she knew that her son was being set up and she and her family were not going to stand for it. No one was going to succeed in using the machinations of some pregnancy to try to trap her son. I maintained my poise and dignity as I left her presence. I had been through enough in the past few weeks to allow the insults that accompanied me as I departed to slide off like water on an oily skin.

I went back to the salon. It was one of our busy afternoons, something I was thankful for, as it took my mind away from my unpleasant encounter with Mrs. Durosimi. It was a lively and jocular group, and I was glad for the temporary distraction, even though a number of things lay heavy on my mind.

Mrs. Jolayemi was getting her hair done at the salon that afternoon, and when she was done, she whispered to me that she would like to see me privately. We went out into the doorway where she went right into the heart of the matter. "People are talking…about the Uchendu girl…in your house." She jerked her head in the direction of the salon to further drive home the point.

It was true that Nneka Uchendu was still with us. I had no objection to this, and neither did Fred. We had both agreed that it was better for her to stay with us than wander the streets aimlessly. Yet I still longed for some reconciliation to happen with her and her family. Fred and I did not return to their house after that first time, but we did send emissaries, who were not successful. I longed for some stability in her life. It was clear that all these made for juicy ingredients to feed the rumor mill, and stories were starting to circulate.

I listened as she continued. "You know, they say she stole—"

I stopped her at this point, and tossing an element of joviality in, I asked laughingly, "Mrs. J, who told you that?'

She seemed a little despondent as she said, "I am only trying to help you. You don't want to start losing your customers because of…" she stopped as she left me to fill in the gaps.

I did not doubt that Mrs. J was trying to help me, and as I linked my arm in hers and led her toward the exit, I reassured her, "You worry too much. Everything is fine."

She gave me a doubtful look and a weak smile and bade me farewell. I realized that the problem had less to do with people gossiping about the Uchendu scandal and more to do with Nneka staying in the house, completely idle. She had stopped going to the university where she had been enrolled and had confided in me that she had no interest in continuing to study. I felt like I had enabled this form of idleness, and even though she helped out in the salon—she was quick on her feet and very resourceful—I knew that the time had come for her to forge a life of her own.

The next day was the Saturday morning market, and I set out early to get some freshly slaughtered cow meat from the abattoir. As I stepped out of the compound, I noticed a figure standing by the corner of the house. Years of living in Lagos had taught me to be vigilant, and even though the shape of the figure seemed feminine, it did not make the intentions less sinister. We were living in desperate times, and both men and women turned to crime. As the figure moved toward me, I realized it was Mrs. Uchendu. My apprehension was replaced by a huge wave of relief as I interpreted her presence to mean that the reconciliation that we had hoped and prayed for was about to happen. I had not seen her since that ill-fated morning when we had gone to their house, and looking at her now, I noticed that her small frame had withered even more. She hesitated as she walked slowly toward me. I moved my basket from my right hand to my left so that I could greet her with a warm embrace, but she gave me a frosty look and went right to her point. "We are going back to the east today," she blurted out. She waited for a reaction from me, which did not come as I tried to process the implication of what she had just said. She may have expected some form of outrage, and when that was not forthcoming, she looked at the ground and then to the sky.

"Nneka should not have stolen." Her voice now took an edgy, serious tone. "That is one thing that her father can never forgive, stealing. It is such a dishonorable thing, especially since we always make sure that she is provided for." My continued silence made her uneasy, but I was determined not to play judge, jury, and executioner.

"I think you..." She stopped talking then, and I saw tears roll down her face. "She can't live with us because of what she did." She started to turn around and paused to whisper: "Tell Nneka I am sorry." It was a very low whisper, and I think she may have said "thank you," but maybe I imagined that.

57

I watched her retreating figure. I wanted to run after her and shake her and tell her to come back to tell her daughter herself that they were going back to the east—whatever that meant. How would I even tell Nneka that? How do you tell someone that her family has abandoned her for some obscure reason? My mind wandered in different directions as I tried to discern what the next mode of action would be. It was the first of two surprises I would receive that morning.

I returned home from the market to discover that we had company. A middle-aged man was seated in our living room, sipping a cup of tea. He jumped to his feet and started, "Madam, please let me apologize for the treatment that you received from my wife." He took my hands in his and squeezed them. I could tell he was nervous, but he was doing a good job of trying to hide it. I vacillated between guilt and elation as I realized that this was Afolabi Durosimi's father. I felt guilty because I had not yet summoned the courage to tell Fred about my clandestine visit to Mrs. Durosimi and elation because this visit translated into an acknowledgment of culpability of the paternity of the child. I tried to hide my emotions by remaining calm.

Mr. Durosimi was uncomfortable, and this was understandable. Fred was seated in his treasured corner of the living room, and I tried to decipher the portions of the conversation that I may have missed. I was wondering why Afolabi himself had not accompanied his father on this visit, when a young man came into the living room from the kitchen with Adesuwa, holding her hand. I bristled and gave Fred a piercing stare. This was the sort of thing that would happen when I was not home. Afolabi offered a greeting, which I ignored. It was wise of him to remain where he was because there was no telling what I would do if he came closer—a kick and a slap were on top of my list. If only Fred were the aggressive kind—the boy would have had a black eye already. But my peace-loving husband had made tea for them. How quaint!

My reaction did not escape Mr. Durosimi, who went on a (clearly preprepared) soliloquy to describe his son as a responsible individual who was very committed to our daughter and was going to do the right thing. I tuned out his words as I tried to size him up. He seemed educated, a little rough around the edges, but perhaps it was the situation he found himself in that made that so. His diction was polished, a good command of English. I looked at Afolabi and Adesuwa standing in solidarity in one corner of the room, him looking like he had been caught stealing sugar, and she trying so hard to be vindicated, both so young and innocent.

Something, perhaps motherly instinct, told me that this visit was just a way to fulfill an obligation. Almost like a tick in the box so that it would not be said that the Durosimis turned their back on Adesuwa Erhabor while she was carrying their son's child.

The meeting with the Durosimis ended with Fred speaking on behalf of our families and saying how this was a time for joy and not for sadness. I could have shot him. Words, all words. What would happen when the time came for action?

I was relieved when they left. It was a brief interlude that I did not need that morning. Adesuwa knew that I was not in the mood to provide any feedback, and she escaped downstairs to the salon, where the Saturday morning rush was about to begin.

I had another mission to accomplish that morning and went in search of Nneka. She had this habit of staying in Adesuwa's bedroom and busying herself with a drawing pad. As I came in, I saw her sketching away. Enitanwa was with her, reading a book. With one look I conveyed to her that her presence was no longer needed, and I sat down next to Nneka. I could read the anxiety and nervousness in her body language as I gently requested to see her drawing pad. She handed it over to me without hesitation, and I was confounded by what I saw. There were pages and pages of designs of dresses and fabric swatches. They were exquisitely done, like something that a professional would do.

"Did you do these?" I asked. She gave a weak nod and then relaxed when I said, "These are very good, Nneka."

She said "Thank you" as I closed the drawing pad and handed it back to her.

"Have you ever thought about going into the fashion business?" I asked. Her affirmative response made me realize that this was something she had thought about often. I already knew the answer to my next question, but I asked it all the same. "Have you spoken to Mercy about this?"

She nodded.

What I said next was not something I had thought about extensively. "How would you like to go and stay with Mercy and her sister for a little while?"

Mercy had just completed her studies in fashion design, and she had expressed an interest in setting up something on her own (no matter how small), rather than engaging in any form of apprenticeship, which was usually the next step for recent graduates in her field. The way I saw it, Mercy had the technical expertise and Nneka had the talent—a gift—divinely endowed. I had seen them together enough times to know that they got along.

I knew that my thinking was aligned with Nneka's when she responded, "That way I can help her as she sets up her fashion design business." She was smiling, and that pleased me, yet I weighed what I had to say next very heavily before I continued. I knew that it would ill behoove me if did not speak, so I went ahead. "Your mother came to see me today. She said they are going back to the east." I waited for this to sink in before going on. "I know that your parents are not happy with you, and I have never asked why because it is not important to me. What I think is important is for you to try to make something for yourself with this life that you have been given. Do not let one single episode direct the course of your life. Who knows; maybe when you excel, you can reconcile with your family and prove that you are not what they think you are." I tried to ignore the tears that were streaming down her face. She started to say something, but I held my hand up to stop her. Words were not necessary. Enough had been said. We held each other in a warm embrace, and I realized that I was crying too as I whispered, "You will be fine, my dear."

Nneka went to live with Mercy and Lilian. Lilian welcomed her with open arms—with Bade's incarceration and his mother's demise, they had moved in with her father-in-law, shortly after she had had her new baby. From what I understood, the senior Mr. Omotosho was not an easy person to get along with, let alone live with, and the more people that Lilian had on her side, the better for her. Within months Nneka and Mercy had set up something small. They came to the salon to hand out their flyers and got some new customers. The feedback I received was always glowing, and even though I kept telling them not to, they always made new outfits for me, which they refused to let me pay for and which I always politely declined. It was not always good business to offer your services free of charge. Their only other option was to give me a highly discounted rate, and I reciprocated with a generous gratuity.

With Nneka settled in the Omotosho household, I felt that one challenge had been temporarily taken care of. It was time to focus on Adesuwa and her pregnancy. My daughter's mental capacity was of vital importance to me, especially when the neighborhood tongues began to wag when her situation became common knowledge. People always found something to talk about, but the last thing I wanted was for my daughter—or my family, for that matter—to collapse under the weight of those whispers. Fred, myself, Fred Junior, Labake, and Enitanwa rallied around her as her support system to let her always be aware that this was a thing of joy and not a source of shame. I think this strengthened her as she grew in her pregnancy. The visit from the Durosimis was the only one we would have until the baby arrived. We heard from them as rarely as rain in the Sahara, but we settled into our lives and the monotonous routine calmly and serenely, waiting with expectant delight for the arrival of the baby, who I secretly hoped would be a girl. Everything seemed planned and directed, and then Reuben showed up.

I always knew that Enitanwa's heart still had a place in the home where she had spent the early part of her life, and this was why I never discouraged her when she was old enough to go and visit her real mother. Although, because I feared for her safety, I often made sure that she did not go unaccompanied, Fred Junior would drive her, but never Fred Senior. I did not want anyone to have any ideas. I had been bitten once, and I was more than a million times shy. She never spoke much about her other siblings but did mention that her older brother, Reuben, often expressed a desire to come to Lagos. He seemed frustrated and stifled living with their mother. She mentioned it a few times, and I did not entertain it; I just responded with my standard refrain: "Pray about it." She must have prayed about it, and those prayers were answered, because one afternoon Reuben showed up. He came to stay, and who better to welcome him with open arms than Fred.

Enitanwa was in school. Adesuwa was taking another one of her long naps. I was in the salon, and Fred was outside reading the paper. He came in to ask for a glass of water, and when I went out to give it to him, I realized he was not alone. It was not until later that evening that I realized Reuben was here to stay. Fred had had a long conversation with him, and he did not give me any details except to let me know that he had nowhere else to go. I was greatly displeased as I considered a situation where Enitanwa's mother would send all her children (and she had many) to live with us. I found this totally unacceptable, but as we prepared for bed that night, Fred tried to reassure me that this was the best thing to do, and only good would come out of it.

Reuben endeared himself to everyone. Fred was his best ally. Since our son had moved out of the house, my husband had been longing for male companionship. Not only did he live in a house full of women, but the bottom floor of his house was always bubbling over with female hormones with the constant traffic of women coming into the salon. The arrival of Reuben was what he needed to reinject some testosterone into our household: someone to play chess with, someone to watch the football league matches with, and someone to talk boring male stuff with. It was now easier for him to tune out the females in the house. Rather than view him as a rival for his father's attentions, my son, Fred, also heralded the arrival of Reuben with bells and whistles, as not only did it take the pressure off him to make the obligatory weekend visit to his father, but it also turned out that Reuben was very useful to Fred Junior and his wife by helping them around the house.

During the final stage of her pregnancy, Adesuwa started to crave garden eggs. Having gone through two pregnancies, I knew how cravings could wreak havoc on a woman's mental stability, and I went to great lengths to try to get them for her. It was no easy feat, and I was stymied in most of my efforts, since garden eggs are a seasonal vegetable and Adesuwa had chosen the time when they were not in season to crave them. However, like a conjurer of illusory magic tricks, Reuben would show up with large baskets of garden eggs. From him I learned to include them in sauces and stews, and before long the whole household was hooked on garden eggs. Enitanwa beamed with delight as she regarded her older brother and his resourcefulness with pride. He had even won over the Mercy-Nneka duo by helping them spread word of their fashion business far and wide and even serving as a delivery boy when they needed to get finished clothes to their customers. He had no interest in going to school like his sister, who was determined to become a lawyer, and told us he did not have a head for the words and numbers in the academic setting. He was happier being skillful in other ways, and with time we accepted this as he became a permanent member of our household.

One rainy Saturday evening, Adesuwa's daughter came screaming into our world. It had been a short labor, and my daughter would later say that the memory of the pain, which was indescribable, had disappeared the moment her child was placed in her arms. Afolabi and his family were notably absent, and we sent Reuben to their house to let them know that there was a new addition to their family. It was a time of gladness and looking forward, and there were no regrets.

Afolabi showed up alone on the day we named the child. He picked up his daughter and held her, and from that moment we could not keep him away from her. His visits, which were infrequent when Adesuwa was expecting, now became annoyingly ceaseless. Our new granddaughter was named Oluwatosin Abieyuwa, and we would all call her Tosin. It is interesting how a tiny child could change everything, and that was exactly what happened. In all the years I had had the salon, I had never taken a single day off, but with Tosin's arrival, I left Mama Yeside in charge and finally took time off.

Grandparenting was not easy for me, first because it had been a while since I had had a baby of my own, and second because Adesuwa was still too young to be a mother. Although the love and nurturing part came naturally, there were certain things that she was still too immature to handle. I had to let her and Afolabi know that the child was not a doll baby that needed to be cuddled and carried; you had to feed and change her and also study her because a child's personality is revealed right from the moment he or she is born. During one particularly annoying incident when both Adesuwa and Afolabi were with Tosin and she kept crying, the more they cuddled her, the more she cried. I could hear them frantically trying to decipher what was wrong with her. Fred had recently chastised me for always being there when Afolabi came around and not giving the two young people a chance to be a couple. It was a very harsh rebuke, which hurt even more, first because it came from Fred and second because he had said it in front of Adesuwa, who had probably been thinking the same thing. After that, anytime Afolabi came around, I excused myself.

On this particular afternoon, I was in the living room reading a magazine while Fred was reading a book on philosophy. The baby's loud cries had disrupted the tranquility in the house, and I could tell that it carried down into the salon, which was busy with customers. From where I sat, I knew what the problem was: the baby's diaper needed to be changed. Yet the two knucklehead parents had no clue and kept on cuddling her.

As the screams grew louder, Fred could not take it anymore. "I think you should go and do something to help them," he said. I found the frustrated sound in his voice amusing and sat for a minute longer without looking up or acting as if what he had just said had been directed at me. He was about to repeat himself when I stood up, went into the room, took the child from her mother, and brought her screaming into the living room, where I changed her diaper. Immediately after that she stopped crying. Her parents had watched in awe, as if I had just performed a magic act.

The next day I invited Lilian Omotosho over to the house, and she and Adesuwa spent hours talking. After that things changed, and Adesuwa was transformed into a more responsible mother; she even started telling me what to do, as she had mastered her daughter's character. I still continued to spend the night in the room with her and Tosin, and that was where I was when the fire started.

I never really discovered what had started the fire. I would later remember that I had heard a sound like breaking glass, but I had been fast asleep and thought I was dreaming. It was the smell that woke me up, and I sat up, still trying to understand what the smell was, when Reuben burst into the room, Fred right behind him. I had never seen the look he had on his face. I heard the words "the house is on fire". Adesuwa shot up and grabbed her baby. Everything was happening so fast. Fraught with fear, we descended to the ground floor, and that was when I felt the rawest form of fear I had ever felt. The entire ground floor was engulfed in flames. As I tried to reach the front door, there was no way; fire was everywhere. Helpless, I looked behind me, where a frightened Adesuwa stood with her baby in her arms. I was trying to figure out what to do next when Reuben appeared with a bucket of water, with which he doused the flames at the front door. The heat clung to us, but we now had an opening to get out, and I quickly pushed Adesuwa out of the door into the street. I was about to turn around and go back in to help with the fire when a strong arm pushed me out into the street. I almost fell on Adesuwa and the baby. I looked behind me to see Reuben; the fire had spread so fast that now there were flames separating us.

By the time Adesuwa and I had scrambled to the other side of the street, we were able to get a full view of the house. The entire ground floor was in flames; it gave a luminous glow to the dark sky. It was when I saw this that I started to scream. The neighbors had already been alerted, and I saw two men rush past us with a large barrel of water. They disappeared into the house. Within a short time, the entire street was abuzz with activity. But Fred, Enitanwa, Reuben—all three of them were still in the house.

I dashed in front of the house and started to shout for people to help me to get my family out of the house. A group of people came out carrying a limp figure. It was Enitanwa, soaking wet, exhausted but unharmed. We carried her and put her on the ground on the other side of the street. Where were Reuben and Fred? By this time there was a huge crowd gathered that I could not see past. Many were scared that the fire would spread to the houses next door. The noise, the smell. Everything was so confusing.

I stood in front of the house and looked at the other side of the street. I could see Adesuwa and Enitanwa, who was now upright. There was someone standing next to them, and I could tell that they were trying to convince them to come into one of the neighbors' houses to rest. I knew my girls enough to know that they would ignore such a plea.

I nudged my way through the crowd and stopped in front of the house. People were milling around me. Water was being brought in containers of different shapes and sizes. In the distance, I could hear the wailing of a siren. Someone was shouting that we should clear away to allow the fire truck to pass through. I stood where I was. A strong arm held me. I did not look past the house. I was praying fervently. "Lord, if you want to, take the house, but give me Fred and Reuben. I cannot live with this on my conscience." I realized I was crying when I looked through my blurry tears and saw that my son, Fred Junior, was the one holding me. Someone must have sent for him.

We both looked helplessly as the firemen declared they did not have enough water in their truck to contain the fire. The heat from the fire, the heaviness of the emotion—it was all too much for me. I fell into Fred Junior's arms. Someone suggested that he take me farther away from the house. The shouting became even more agitated. Someone was coming out. I stood upright. The firemen were leading one figure out. Fred? Reuben? Fred Junior left me and went toward the house. Someone was shouting that water should be brought. There were women around me whose voices I recognized, but in the chaos I could not figure out who they were. They were the ones who held me back from going after my son. I swore I heard Fred's voice. As I looked closer, I noticed that the figure that had been led out was carrying another figure on its back. I watched as Fred Junior helped his father lift Reuben off his back. I closed my eyes and said a prayer of thankfulness.

I had been joined by Adesuwa, Enitanwa, and Labake. Tosin was nestled on her mother's back, fast asleep, and oblivious to all the noise and chaos around her. We moved closer. Fred had a huge cut on his right leg. He looked frazzled and worn-out. Reuben still lay on the ground. He was having a huge coughing fit, which someone was giving him water for. I sat next to him. And we all looked at the house. It had burned to the ground. The plaintive cries of sympathy around us made me realize the true impact of what we had just gone through. We had lost everything in the fire, but we still had each other. We were all safe and sound.

We ended up in Fred Junior's house that night. A lot had changed. The smell of the fire would reside in my nostrils for days. Even though I did not have any visible physical injuries, I felt the intensity of the heat from the fire nestled in my body and would feel that way for years. Labake, who had a fancy word to describe many things, would call it *post-traumatic stress syndrome* and even had the effrontery to suggest that I seek medical help for it. My response was a piercing gaze. After the fire, we strived to settle into some pattern of normalcy as we came to terms with what had happened. The very next morning after the incident, our first visitor was Afolabi, who had received the shock of his life when he had arrived at our place for his daily visit with his child only to discover the charred remains of the house. Neighbors who directed him to Fred Junior's place had reassured him that everyone had been able to get out unharmed. Upon confirming that we were indeed safe and sound, he disappeared. He returned a few hours later, accompanied by his parents, who came shrouded in shame and guilt. My second encounter with Mrs. Durosimi was a far cry from the first. Caught between a rock and a hard place, she arrived with bundles of supplies for the newborn child and us. I was surprised to learn that it would be the first time she was meeting not only baby Tosin but also Adesuwa. It took a fire to bring her off her high horse. But life is like that sometimes; a drastic and sadly sometimes tragic situation often reminds us how fragile we really are. Many people would remind us how lucky we were that all of us including a newborn child just beginning to carve her existence on this earth had escaped unscathed.

The one person whose change I was not prepared for was Fred's. I had always considered my husband's passive amaranthine strength to be one of his greatest gifts. He had been self-sufficient for years, especially as I worked full-time in the salon, but now it seemed like he was just as helpless as his granddaughter, needing to be waited on constantly. At first I thought he had been hurt in the fire, but as I looked closer, I realized that he had aged by a dozen years since the fire, something no one was prepared for.

The other thing that I was not prepared for was the fact that the family would need to be separated. Fred had a smaller place, which meant that we could not all comfortably fit in. Adesuwa, Enitanwa, and the baby moved in with Lilian, Mercy, and Nneka. They were all already spending more time there during the day as they helped out with the fashion business. Papa Omotosho had uncharacteristically invited Fred and me to move in with him, and we had politely declined, even though our girls were next door to him.

We received so many gestures of kindness after the fire. Yet nothing prepared me for the greatest gift of all. Someone who chose to remain anonymous had offered to rebuild the entire house for free. We had no idea who it was, and the more we asked, the less we heard. All we were told was to sit back and relax and all would be taken care of, and it was. There is a proverb that says: "When the king's palace burns down, the rebuilt palace is more beautiful," and that was what happened to us. We got a new house, built on the same place where the original Terra-Cotta Beauty stood, but much more modern than I could have imagined. We did not know who to thank for this gift, but I did know that the time had now come for me to prepare to pass on the baton to the next generation.

It is late now, and my eyes are losing the battle with time, so sometimes I need help seeing things. I think the most important thing when you get to be my age is to look back and be at peace with yourself. Peace with the choices and decisions that you made, contentment with the things you did not do. In many ways I often look at my life in two stages, before and after the fire. We lost everything we had worked for in the fire, but I think of all the things that we did not lose in the fire, and that makes me happy. The fire helped as a jolt to reality to show me how much stronger we were collectively.

Yesterday I went to vote for the first time in my life. I voted for a man whose name is Goodluck and whom everyone seems to think is the one who will bring much-needed hope to our country. Time will tell. Although it was the first time I voted, it was not the first time we had had elections to choose our president. During the first set of elections, I was out of the country. Fred had fallen ill all of a sudden. It was Fred Junior's suggestion that we seek medical treatment overseas. He and Labake had moved to the United States to study but decided that they preferred life there to life at home, and now I have American grand-children who have to speak slowly so that I can understand them. Fred was diagnosed with prostate cancer. We had left it too long and it had spread to other parts of his body. Within a year he was gone. I think part of me left with him. You expect these things to happen—it is the circle of life, but you are never really ready for it when it does happen. We brought him back home and buried him beside his sister. I moved back into the living space above the salon. Surrounded by Fred's books and the ambiance in the house that had been rebuilt for us, I found peace.

Fewer things surprised me more than the fact that Adesuwa and Afolabi Durosimi got married. I realized that there is truth in first love being the lasting love. It took a while for my daughter to forgive him for his unexplained absence during her pregnancy and the birth of their daughter, and he pursued her relentlessly until she succumbed. Fred and I were pleased to see them wed. There was still no love lost between our two families, though there remained some form of cordi-ality between us, but for the most part we kept to ourselves and left our children to live their lives with our blessings.

Enitanwa became a lawyer. A very good one, very much sought after. Her mission in Lagos over, she set up a practice in the small town of her birth and fought for the rights of the people, giving a voice to those who would otherwise have none. I felt a deep sense of pride when I read about her in the papers. For years I had carried the guilt of separating a child from her mother, and now I felt vindicated. She was doing what she had been called to do.

Her brother, Reuben, never left Lagos. He never left the salon. After the fire, when the house was being rebuilt, a smaller house was constructed for him behind the main house and he evolved into having the managerial role and overseeing the salon when it became too much for me to handle with Fred's illness. He engaged in other business ventures on the side: spare parts for cars, computers. Once anything new was emerging, he was always the source for it. I still did not know how he managed, but he never got into any trouble, so it all seemed above board.

Many of the people who originally worked with me in the salon stayed after the house was rebuilt, but with time they would also depart, to be replaced by other people. Mama Yeside remained with us until arthritis got the better of her hands and she was not able to plait hair like she used to. Her daughters had grown into capable young women, and, although much to their mother's chagrin, neither of them went into the salon business, they stepped into the reverse role of looking after her.

Pride is a terrible thing, especially among family members, and it played a large part in Nneka Uchendu never reconciling with her family. We learned that her sister had joined a convent. I never saw her parents again. I never heard even so much as a whisper from them. Nneka and Mercy remained in business together. Their fashion outfit became very successful at home and abroad. They became famous for what they were able to do with our local *ankara* fabric, and though many came after them, following the same fashion technique, they remained the pioneers, and their creations graced international runways. Mercy got married and started a family, and Nneka continued to remain single. The betrayal she had experienced so young in her life would remain a scar emblazoned on her heart, and she never let anyone in.

Bade Omotosho languished in prison for many years. The resistance movement he had helped to start became a large thorn in the flesh of the military. They had no choice but to allow full-fledged democracy to take root in our country, and the military returned to the barracks. Shortly after the exit of the military, Bade was released from prison. We were thankful that his father lived to see him come out of his unjust imprisonment and Papa Omotosho died peacefully in his sleep later that year. Bade's long stay in prison had made him develop all sorts of health issues, the type our rudimentary public health system was not able to handle. His health was deteriorating rather badly and it was decided that it would be better for them to live abroad where his health could be better taken care of. Lilian would go on to study for a doctorate degree and enter the realms of European academia. It was a sad irony that Bade was unable to live in the democracy that he had fought so hard and sacrificed so much for.

It is late, and my eyes are not as young as they used to be, but I can still see how bright the future is.

Iridescent Hope

S he smelled it before she saw it, and the large flies that were beginning to circle her head in the morning sun confirmed what it was
as they led her in a procession toward it. At first she thought it was the
corpse of some animal that had been knocked down by a careless driver, but as she drew closer she realized what it was. She gasped loudly,
instantly covering her mouth before one of the flies could decide to
take a trip down her throat.

The charred remains of a human being lay several feet away from
her. As she walked rapidly past it, she had to fight the human curiosity to gape at the remains of the dead person while trying as hard as
possible not to gag as the putrid smell jolted her senses to life and
threatened to eject the contents of her stomach.

Without looking, she tried to cross to the other side of the dirt
road as thoughts whirled through her head. She confirmed to herself
that the body that lay there now had not been there when she had
walked down this same road the previous day on her way back from
work. The loud honk of a horn startled her momentarily as she realized that she had stopped in the middle of the street. Tears stung her
eyes as the *okada* driver and his passenger—a young man clutching a
manila folder while balancing steadily on the back of the motorcycle—
cursed at her simultaneously. Their voices faded into the morning air,
and as she approached the bus stop she realized that she was sobbing
loudly. Almost immediately she heard the steady stream of a familiar
tune from one of the ramshackle stalls that dotted the bus stop, and
she laughed out loud as she recognized the upbeat melody of Onyeka
Onwenu's "One Love." She wondered whose corpse it was that she had

seen lying so ordinarily on the street on a weekday morning, whether it was male or female. Probably male, probably an accused thief who had fallen victim to the *jungle justice* meted out recklessly by young people in the city, often catalyzed by the howls of *"Ole o!" "Ole o!"*

Several minutes later she boarded the staff bus at the regular pickup point to transport her and her colleagues to their workplace on the island off the mainland. She still could not get the image out of her mind and resolved to take the longer walk home to avoid seeing it, all the while asking her Creator to rest the soul of whoever it was who had suffered such an indignity.

She began to focus her attention on the day that lay before her. She had a lot to be thankful for. A number of people would do anything to be in the position that she held as the personal assistant to the head of human resources at a well-established and successful commercial bank. Yet, she knew that she was nothing less than a glorified errand girl. Mrs. Kalu was the head of human resources and Olawunmi's boss. Unfortunately, there was nothing human about her. Her words and her actions had such a pulverizing effect on even the most resilient spirit that you had to have a high level of emotional stamina in order to resist being scathed by her. During her first week on the job, Olawunmi had cringed as she listened to a telephone conversation between Mrs. Kalu and one of the branch managers in another part of the country who was seeking reimbursement for medical expenses incurred when his wife had a complicated delivery that required additional surgical interventions. Mrs. Kalu, confirming from the man that this was their fifth child, proceeded to give him a thorough lecture on family planning, going as far as accusing him of being one of the many men who was overpopulating the country.

Following that initial experience, Olawunmi would spend the next three years acquiring a great deal of ambidexterity in her role. It was a necessary skill, combined with the patience and tact that was required to put out the conflagrations that were inevitably lit as a result of her boss's obvious intolerance for people. Her boss's nuances and quirks were given the summary title "Mrs. Kalu's *wahala*." Nobody was prepared to deal with this metaphorical *wahala*, which was almost like a saber-toothed tiger tearing up everything in its way and leaving people with the lowest form of self-esteem imaginable. All the while condemning them to episodes of nail biting and teeth gnashing. If possible it was avoided like a plague, and most people eased themselves out of situations where they would have to confront it.

As the image of the dead body she had seen early that morning managed to shadow her thoughts during most of the day, Olawunmi busied herself with her work. Most days consisted of following instructions barked at her by her vixen of a boss and pacifying a number of people who had been rubbed the wrong way by Mrs. Kalu and her *wahala*. There was a wide range, from those in the headquarters to those in the branch offices, who would ceaselessly burn the phone lines with one story of infraction or the other. The only time she felt she could exhale unperturbed was when Mrs. Kalu finally left the confines of the office suite they shared to attend a management meeting. Then Olawunmi felt free to stretch all thirty-four inches of her legs under her desk. Later that day, she was summoned into Mrs. Kalu's office when the latter returned with the news that the fleet of staff buses—a well-received perk that helped to assuage the commuting woes of a high percentage of the headquarters staff—was being yanked away from the beneficiaries in the most sudden and unexpected manner.

The fact was that the city of Lagos was undergoing a crippling fuel crisis, and it was becoming increasingly difficult for the bank to continue to justify buying fuel at exorbitant prices for the buses, all of which were assigned to various routes on the mainland part of the city. It was for this reason that senior management had decided to pull the buses off the roads until the fuel crisis had dissipated and things were back to normal. The staff buses would, with immediate effect be parked on the premises of the bank, and staff members (Olawunmi included) who relied on the staff bus for the commute home from work would have to find other ways to commute. Olawunmi had the unmerited pleasure of drafting the memo and also bearing the brunt of the insults meted out by her colleagues, who demanded a more detailed explanation since none of the members of senior management were relinquishing the company cars assigned to them.

The truth was that the senior management could care less, since they had little or nothing to do with the staff bus. If a member of that group had showed the slightest form of compassion for the plight of the people who relied on the staff bus, it was clear that he or she would have borne the full weight of Mrs. Kalu's *wahala*. The announcement was made on a Friday evening, and everyone found their way home with whatever means they could that evening.

The following Monday, several colleagues met to swap stories of what they had to endure during their commute to work. Pius Anyiam, a brilliant yet dull and unassuming character in the Accounting department, swore that he had seen one of the staff buses in his neighborhood early on Sunday morning with the banner of an evangelical church concealing the familiar acronyms of the bank that had been emblazoned on the side of the bus. Standing a short distance away from the group, Olawunmi shook her head in disbelief. It was possible that she was the only one present who knew that Mrs. Kalu and her husband were the grand patron and patroness of that particular church and that only that past weekend the church had held its annual prayer meeting. People from all over the country had convened at the church's headquarters, located smack in the middle of a densely populated area of the mainland, which just happened to be the neighborhood where Pius Anyiam lived. She was not wrong in her suspicions that Mrs. Kalu had used the staff bus in order to convey people attending this prayer meeting to the destination, especially considering that the perceptive Mr. Anyiam described the vigorousness with which the occupants of the bus had belted out popular praise and worship hymns.

Olawunmi herself had had a grueling ordeal commuting to work that morning. There were fewer commuter buses plying the roads at this point of the fuel crisis. She had ambled to the bus stop, this time taking the longer route in order to avoid having to encounter the body, which she had heard from people in recent days was still lying languidly on the side of the road. Unlike previous days when she waited for her staff bus at the makeshift bus stop that was far from the madness of the crowd, she had had to mingle with the throngs of people who waited for the commercial vehicles that would take them to their various destinations. The word *chaos* took on another meaning and dimension of its own. It became clear the extent the fuel crisis had reached when the familiar *danfo* buses were a rare sight, as most of them ran on petrol that had become a precious commodity in town. The only form of transportation that was visible that morning was the black and yellow- mammoth-shaped bus that had been given the incomparable name *molue*.

There was nothing else like it in Lagos, and for many commuters that morning it was a godsend because it ran on diesel. At that point of the fuel crisis, diesel had not fallen into the ranks of what were considered essential but scarce commodities. Yet many cynics were quick to point out that it was just a question of time, since word on the street was that the scarcity was about to extend to diesel.

In the meantime *molues* were the saving grace for Lagos commuters relying on public transportation. If you were yet to master the art of jumping on a *molue* in motion, it was a good time to learn. *Molue* jumping was an art that a fair share of the commuting population in Lagos—old and young, male and female—had mastered to an impeccable tee. Olawunmi tried not to look too astounded as she watched a young mother with her infant strapped diligently to her back run quickly, catch a *molue* in motion, and hold on for dear life, squeezing herself through the throng of people at the entrance. She braced herself, thinking that if that young woman could do it, there was no reason why she could not.

Well aware that in this crowd could be nestled one or two predatory pickpockets, she held her handbag and her larger tote bag, which contained her decent work shoes and a number of items she would need to freshen up when she got into work. She followed the singsong voice that screamed "CMS! CMS!" and made her first futile attempt to board the *molue*. It was almost like magic; the crowd of people that had a moment ago been subdued suddenly came to life, and everyone leaped toward the large behemoth of a vehicle. A rotund man with a tie sticking out of his shirt pocket shoved her aside as she tried to retain her equilibrium. Someone else pushed her, and in the middle of this she saw one of the slippers she had on slide off her feet in the opposite direction of the rush. Hopping on one foot, she tried to go after her runaway slipper. As the crowd pushed and shoved her from one side to the other, she did not lose sight of it, and she finally managed to put her one nude foot into the rubbery shoe, catching her breath and looking in the direction of the receding vehicle. Even as the vehicle moved faster, more and more people tried to get into it. One young man reeled forward and jumped on, only to be jettisoned off because he could not hold on tightly enough.

And almost immediately it started; the madness was over, and all that was left was the ebbing of the singsong voice of the conductor of the *molue* still calling on passengers to board for central Lagos, even when it was obvious that the bus was full to capacity. In its wake the *molue* had added to litter on the busy street—a pair of matching Dunlop slippers, a baby's well-used feeding bottle, and several oranges that were now being snatched off the ground by children who seemed to appear from nowhere—reminders of what had just transpired. She resolved to get on the next *molue* to CMS even if it meant she had to lose all the dignity that she had built up for herself in all her years of grooming as an adult.

Two *molues* later she found herself in one, standing conscious of everyone around and nursing a sharp pain in her toes, which she longed to caress but could not because there was standing room only. She was sure that if she even tried to bend, everyone else would lose their balance and curse her for it. A wide variety of smells on the *molue* made her feel sick; the interior of the bus reeked of some stench that was a combination of dampness and degradation.

By the time she sat at her desk that morning, she had spent enough time freshening up that there was not even a trace of her commuting ordeal. When Mrs. Kalu arrived two hours later than the rest of the staff, she was able to welcome her with a smile plastered on her face and a warm greeting and customary curtsy. The latter replied by looking her straight in the eye, scanning her appearance from head to toe and nodding a response. During lunch with her friend Uloma later that day, Olawunmi narrated her ordeal to her in as graphic a manner as possible, highlighting the details, while Uloma chuckled loudly in between mouthfuls of food. Uloma, who worked for a smaller organization without a staff bus, elected to remind Olawunmi that the ordeal that she insisted on griping about was the commuting reality for not too few people.

"Let me introduce you to another way of coming to work," Uloma said with a twinkle in her eye in response to Olawunmi's question of how she managed in the face of the commuting dilemma many were faced with. "The ferry."

The puzzled look on her friend's face made Uloma laugh out loud, as she explained that there were actually ferries located in strategic parts of Lagos that transported workers from the mainland to the island. They were not as common as the *molues* or the *danfos*, but they did exist.

It was Uloma's idea that Olawunmi spend the weekdays with her in the home that she shared with her cousin in Festac Town, which was closer to the ferry terminal, so as to ease her commuting woes. At first Olawunmi was hesitant, not because she did not think of it as a valid offer and one that she felt would make her life a lot easier, but because of the Zuby issue.

Zuby was short for Azubike. He was Uloma's cousin, whom she shared her living space with. His family who owned the house had immigrated to the United States, and the only reason he had been unable to join them was because his two applications for entry visas had been rejected. While he nursed the wounds of the double rejection, he concocted a scheme to get the passport of a neighboring West African country and try to apply from a US consulate over there. The problem with Zuby was that his mind had taken permanent residence in the gutter. If there was anything lewd or lascivious to be said, he said it. He prided himself on being able to say the word *sex* in twelve different languages, a feat he was sure no one else he knew of could boast of. He was willing and ready to share this knowledge with all the girls he met as a pickup line.

The first time that Olawunmi had visited Uloma in her home in Festac Town, she had been stunned with disbelief at the words that he uttered while she waited for her friend, who was getting dressed in her bedroom. Not content to describe his desire in words, he had produced a magazine with images of topless women and couples in various coital positions, which he assured her was her destiny with him. Wide-eyed, Olawunmi was trying to summon all the rage that was building up in her when Uloma emerged and gave Zuby a stern warning, which only emboldened him to snicker in the ugliest manner imaginable. He winked at Olawunmi, blowing her kisses in the air and letting her know his feelings. Later they had laughed it off as Uloma explained the incident away, saying that Zuby was the devil's workshop, the product of an idle mind that did nothing all day but wait for a stipend from Western Union from his absent parents while cooking up schemes to go to America. It had managed to discourage Olawunmi from making any other attempts to visit Uloma at her home.

When she voiced her reason for hesitating to take up Uloma's offer—Zuby's wanton display of affection—the latter was quick to dismiss this. She concluded that Zuby was harmless. Responding to the puzzled stare that Olawunmi gave her, she proceeded to give Olawunmi an account of how Zuby had been trying out his charms on a local girl who sold oranges on the street corner. Unlike many females who spurned his bawdy advances, this girl actually took up Zuby's offer to rock her world. The two had been locked in Zuby's bedroom for close to an hour when the orange seller had exited, raining abuses on Zuby and letting anyone in the neighborhood who cared to listen know that Zuby was all mouth and no action and was nothing more than a dog who chases a car but does not know how to start the engine. So the Zuby issue was laid to rest.

The following day, well versed in the art of *molue* jumping and this time armed with an additional bag of clothes for the week, Olawunmi had left the house she shared with her widowed mother and younger sisters and taken the first *molue* into Lagos Island. In the evening the commute from work to Uloma's place was simplified by the assistance of a Good Samaritan who had given the two young ladies a ride to Uloma's house. It was not until the next day that she would experience her first ferry ride into Lagos.

The ferry terminal was on the stretch of road called the Lagos-Badagry Expressway, which took you from Mile Two toward one of the borders between Nigeria and the Republic of Benin, past the town of Badagry. It was tucked in a corner of the Mile Two bus stop, a short distance away from the madness of the bus stop and the interstate motor park, but bestowed with its own special brand of madness. You could get a good view of the ferry terminal if you stood at the section of the expressway where the interstate night buses parked in a place called Maza Maza.

Zuby was fast asleep on the sofa in the living room as Uloma and Olawunmi left the house. They walked down from the first entry gate into Festac Town toward the ferry terminal. During their walk to the terminal, Uloma attributed his ordeal to the pride and stubbornness of his parents, especially his father, who insisted that the young man join the rest of the family in the United States against all odds, rather than take the advice of various friends and relatives, who advocated he enroll in an institution of higher learning in Nigeria.

As they approached the ferry terminal, Olawunmi noticed that the passengers who were scattered around the terminal were not quite different from those who used what she termed regular transport. There were schoolchildren, some of their faces still dusty with white powder which their mothers had used to make their faces less shiny, and the odd male office worker with a bored look as he tried to appear unnoticeable, especially as two young ladies approached. For many young men, it was not a thing of pride to be seen taking public transport, least of all the ferry, which was lowest in hierarchy of commuting options. Most of the potential passengers were market women encumbered by their merchandise of various shapes, sizes, and odors, which hit the olfactory lobes with an unforgiving fierceness. Closer scrutiny of the setting revealed a ferry boat with some inscription on it indicating that the service was operated by the Lagos state government. This did nothing to calm Olawunmi's anxieties as she tried to inspect the vehicle as much as she could to make sure that water was not leaking into it from underneath. She had nursed fears of the ferry boat sinking in the middle of the Lagos lagoon ever since Uloma had told her about it, and not even the most calming thoughts or memories she tried to muster could shake off those fears.

A man who she assumed was in charge was having an argument with a woman whom he wanted to charge an additional fare because of the weight of her baggage. It took Olawunmi a while to understand that they were waiting for the ferry boat captain. He eventually showed up a short while later, a well-used chewing stick dangling from his lips like it was a part of his anatomy. As he spoke Olawunmi marveled at the fact that the chewing stick stayed in between his lips; even though it moved, there did not seem to be the slightest chance that it would fall to the ground. With a swift move of his hand, the man she had seen arguing with the lady indicated that it was time to board. That was when she noticed that there was already someone on the ferry boat—a younger lad who could not have been more than fifteen, he was the one who let the crowd in. Disorder was everywhere, but it was organized disorder since everyone who was boarding the ferry boat was quite aware that with one false move, anyone of them could fall into the lagoon below. Uloma and Olawunmi had hardly spoken as the latter took in the scene at the ferry terminal and they joined the rest of the throng poised to enter the ferry. The lad who was already on the ferry boat took charge of collecting the fare from the passengers before they boarded, and the two ladies managed to find a seat together. Olawunmi sat saying a silent prayer of protection, which was interrupted by a loud droning noise as the engine of the boat started.

From where she sat, she could see the murky ferry waters lick the base of the boat, and she caught a glimpse of the captain, who was now wearing a brass-rimmed pair of sunglasses. He steered the boat with one slow circular motion of his left hand easing it into the water while shouting a spontaneous phrase to a group of youth gathered on the quay, who responded with a singular gesticulation.

Olawunmi was beginning to relax in her thoughts and muster some level of confidence in the journey, when a voice broke the solemnity. A man dressed in a threadbare suit threw a lukewarm greeting to the crowd gathered on the boat. He introduced himself as a "minister for Christ" and proceeded to say a prayer over the boat, calling on all the lost souls to accept the message of salvation he was preaching. His approach was brash and abrasive as he used graphic and uncouth examples of the wickedness of man, most of it focusing on adultery and fornication, using passages from the Bible to buttress his point. By the time she had gotten the full gist of his message, Olawunmi allowed her mind to wander again. Conversation with Uloma was impossible given the combination of the loud diatribe of the "minister" and incessant drone of the boat's engine.

A small puddle had gathered in a corner of the boat. She had noticed it when she had sat down and at first thought it was a confirmation of her fear that the boat had a leak underneath it. When the level of the puddle remained the same, she realized that perhaps it was the residue from some other trip the boat had taken down the lagoon. As the morning sun caressed the boat, some of its rays hit the puddle, giving it an iridescent shimmer, and as she gazed at it, she felt a surge of hope build up in her. She thought about her life and how she had been left to care for her mother and younger sisters since their father's untimely demise, which was the result of a nameless illness. Her role as breadwinner had been an uncontested reality as she completed the mandatory national youth service and was counted lucky to be able to have snapped up what many termed an enviable position in a bank.

Her mind was still on this journey as she thought about Zuby and wondered how he could live such a banal existence, holding on to some dream of joining his family in a land where perhaps he believed that all the things he wished and hoped for would come to pass. Her mind came to rest on the body she had seen rotting on the street. She imagined that it was some mother's son whose life had come to an end in the most depraved way conceivable. As these thoughts colored her mind, she still felt that sense of hope that all was not lost. Later, when the boat pulled up to the pier at CMS, she actually caught herself smiling, perhaps out of relief for having survived the journey or the knowledge that she could survive anything that was thrown at her at this point in her life. The voices and the smell heralded her arrival to the central part of Lagos Island as she and Uloma joined the passengers who disembarked onto the pier.

Running in the Wrong Direction

*T*hey arrived in Lagos at night; by the time they descended from the back of the truck, every bone in his body ached, and his muscles were sore. He was told that they were in the middle of central Lagos. Balogun Market. This did not really mean anything to him; he was tired and he was hungry. He followed the group as they made their way through a darkened section in the middle of the market. He had no idea where he was; he could barely see. Voices around him of different pitches were speaking a mixture of languages: Igbo, Pidgin English, and Yoruba.

They stopped in front of a poorly lit stall. The older man of the group, who had been their chaperone, informed them that this was their final destination. The other boys crouched on the hard concrete floor, and he did the same. As the youngest in the group, he looked to them for guidance. He fell asleep to the sound of his stomach rumbling and mosquitoes buzzing in his ear. A calm, steady breeze was the only thing that gave him the slightest bit of comfort.

They woke up the next morning at the crack of dawn. Without much ado they had a prayer session that was preceded by them singing worship songs in different languages. Prayers were said by another man, who he would later learn was the older brother of the man who had chaperoned them from Lagos. The other boys called him Uncle, and he did the same. In the morning light, he was able to assess his surroundings better, and he recognized that they were indeed in the middle of a market. Uncle sold electronic appliances, and there were more gadgets in the shop than he had seen in his entire life. It was a wide range, from stereo players to microwave ovens.

He was still poring over them when one of the older boys knocked him on the head, handed him a broom, and commanded him to start sweeping. When he was done, he was charged with going to buy breakfast. He wanted to make a good impression because he knew that this was the only way that he would be able to move up. He would later learn that Uncle had five shops in different locations in which a variety of items were sold.

The day came to an end very fast; he was not sure what his duties were but was ready to do anything and everything that he was asked. In the evening two of the boys who had been part of the group that he had come to Lagos with left. They claimed that they had relatives in the city and went off to find them. At least it was better than sleeping in front of the shop in the open air, at the mercy of mosquitoes and the evil spirits that chose the cover of darkness to roam around and do their evil work. He and the others who did not have any relatives took their chances and resumed their positions from the previous night.

When the other two came back for work the next morning, they looked clean and refreshed. The rest of them had had to endure the indignity of bathing with rationed water in a dark hidden corner of the market.

He spent his days and nights in the market. He learned to ignore the mosquitoes that buzzed in his ears at night and the fact that he was always hungry. When his body temperature started to rise, he ignored that too, focusing instead on the errands that he had to run for Uncle and his other duties.

One evening at closing time, Uncle rounded up all the boys and gave them money. It must have been the end of the month. He should have been excited at receiving his first paycheck, like the other boys, who were counting the money and licking their fingers in order to make sure the notes did not stick together, but by this time he was very sick.

Uncle directed him to a chemist around the corner where he could buy medicine for what was obviously a serious case of malaria. When he got to the chemist, the young boy at the counter, who looked about his age, took one look at him and gave him a small bottle of Lucozade, to give him energy. He sat and gulped it down hurriedly. The boy gazed at him curiously and asked him some pointed questions, starting with where he spent his nights.

He explained his predicament to him, and the latter shook his head. He offered to give him a place to stay. At first he was hesitant. He may have been naïve, but he had heard enough of Lagos to know that predators and their accomplices were hanging around, ready to use people for ritual money-making schemes.

The expression on his face must have revealed the doubts he was entertaining, because his companion said tactlessly, "*Stay there, y'hear! Na all the money wey dem dey pay you wey you go dey use buy melaysin*" ("Keep doing what you are doing. You will use all the money you get paid to buy medicines!")

The point his new friend made was driven home when he realized that more than half of the money he had just been paid had gone to the purchase of the anti-malarial medicines he needed to make him feel better.

The boy introduced himself as Tonye. He had lived in Lagos for more than a year now. When he had first arrived, he too had been an *asunta* (someone who sleeps outside) but that had lasted for less than a month, and now he had his own place, which he shared with a few friends.

They took a bus to a place called Aguda. He was too tired, and the medicine was making him drowsy, so he just nodded and smiled as Tonye introduced him to the others. He counted eight boys. When it was time for them to sleep, their number had increased to eleven. They went into a small room with a narrow bed that took up most of the space. He chose a spot near Tonye on the floor and noticed that none of the other boys went to sleep on the only bed in the room. When he mentioned this to Tonye, he was told that the bed was for Oga Paulinus, who was the original tenant of the room. He worked in a beer parlor and kept late nights. Oga Paulinus's arrival in the wee hours of the morning was accompanied by the strong stench of alcohol.

Hours later, when they were on the bus on the way to the market, Tonye reminded him not to forget that he was going to pay him five hundred naira for the month so that he could pay Oga Paulinus. He would later find out from the other boys that Tonye actually paid Oga Paulee (as they liked to call him) three hundred naira and kept the rest for himself as commission.

If the others at the shop noticed his absence from their nocturnal sleeping arrangement, they did not show it or talk about it. Everyone went about their work with the same kind of mechanical rhythm they had adopted from the moment they had arrived in Lagos. His new commute meant that he would have to wake up earlier and catch the bus.

Tonye did not always spend the night in the room; he had a woman on the other side of town, and on the nights that he needed to, he went to her. When Tonye was not around, he chatted with another boy called Aloy. He did not really like talking to Aloy because he was older and tried to throw his weight around by making condescending remarks. He also smoked heavily, and the cigarette smell hung like an albatross around his neck.

It was during one of his chats with Aloy, when he mentioned that he would like to explore other potential sources of income, that the latter put the clandestine proposition before him. At first he had declined. It was true that he was desperate for money, but still that did not mean he needed to stoop to a criminal level. It was when Aloy, telling him how much he would make in one deal, questioned his manhood and sanity that he started to give it some thought. He told Aloy to give him till the next day to think about it, and the latter extracted a promise from him not to mention their chat to anyone else in the room.

Something happened the next morning that helped him make up his mind. At this point Uncle had developed a certain level of trust in him and often sent him on errands to the bank to deposit small amounts of money. At the bank that morning, his usual teller, a kind, middle-aged man, was not there; in his place was a younger lady with an obnoxious air. She looked at him from head to toe before taking the money he had come to deposit. He was taken aback by the nasty and offhand manner with which she treated him. It was not in his character to deliberately offend people, and while she counted the money, he resolved to somehow be polite to her before she left. Perhaps this would change her attitude.

He asked her what time it was, and the response stung him badly.

"Be asking me what time it is. Your mates are in school; you are standing here asking me what time it is." She hissed loudly, turned on her heel, and walked away without answering his question.

He walked out of the bank, dejected and forlorn.

Granted, it was not the first time someone had been unnecessarily unkind to him since he arrived in Lagos, but it was the first time that there had been a blatant reference to his circumstances. He, alone, knew what his goals were and what he expected to accomplish. He did not need to be reminded in such a harsh tone that things were not exactly what they needed to be.

That night Tonye, who always had a listening ear, was not available for him to pour his heart out to. He could not tell Aloy, who would only make the situation worse by seizing the opportunity to mock him. Instead he told Aloy that he would go with him, provided that, like he had promised, there would be no bloodshed. They would go in and come out with what they needed. End of story. It was just business. He needed to do this to make some extra cash. He said it to himself enough times that he believed it completely.

That weekend he avoided Tonye and snuck out with Aloy to meet the rest of the team members in the den of thieves. The others sized him up and told him what they expected him to do. If he breathed a word of this to anyone else, he should know that he was finished. Aloy vouched for him, claiming he had known him since they were children and he was not that type. He adopted the swagger that was similar to the way Aloy and Tonye carried themselves so as to mingle easily with the group of thugs. Still, it all felt so phony.

There were five of them in total, assigned with various tasks as part of the operation. The plan was for them to carry out their operation the following weekend. There would be guns, but not a shot would be fired. They would just hold them to scare the victims into obeying them.

When he saw the guns, he was scared, but he tried not to show it. It was a fear that he would carry with him for the rest of the week, as thoughts of the pending operation overcame him. Even Uncle noticed that something was wrong and asked him if he had malaria again.

Tonye kept on asking him to tell him what the deal was with his recently acquired taciturnity and faraway looks. At one point he was tempted to tell him everything, but he was too far gone to be able go back or share it with anyone. Aloy would never let him hear the last of it. He was ashamed but convinced himself that this was just a stepping stone for him to be able to accomplish some of the things he had outlined for himself when he came to Lagos. He was not going to make a career out of it.

The gang of thieves all assembled at the meeting place on a hot, balmy Saturday morning. The Nigerian Super Eagles were playing the team from Zambia, and most of the boys from the room had gone to watch the match anywhere that they could, insofar as there was a standby generator that would serve as the perfect solution to the imminent power outages that could disrupt their viewing. His heart pounded as they piled into the car and drove toward their destination. The instructions had been clear, and he had rehearsed his role a million times; he could play it in his sleep. The house was just as had been described; they had dropped him off a few houses away. By the time he walked stealthily into the compound, trying to look like an innocent pedestrian, the operation was already in full swing. His heart was beating fast, and he felt all the blood in his body rush to his head as he went to the ground-floor apartment as instructed. He saw Aloy, who gave him the signal and disappeared to the top-floor apartment as planned.

The occupant of the apartment was an older lady. She lay prostrate on the floor, and he could hear her whispering prayers under her breath. He sat on the sofa in the living room. He was not quite sure what to do. He did not like the way he saw the older woman. He cleared his throat and mustered the courage before he told her to rise to her feet. He knew the instructions were not to let her out of his sight, but at least he could still keep an eye on her if she was upright.

She stood up slowly, wiping her face with her wrapper. She looked at him and gasped. "You are just a child."

A mixture of shame and indignation made him spit back abrasively, "You will see my red eye if you talk again o."

She waited a few more minutes before she said something else. "Are you a Christian?" she asked softly.

This time he decided to ignore her.

There was a momentary pause. He did not expect her to do what she did next. She started to recite Psalm 23, in Yoruba, in a personalized way, directed at him. "The Lord is your shepherd, you shall not want…"

By the time she was through, he could hear his heart pounding through his ears. He did not know he was crying until he tasted the salt of the tears that were now streaming down his face. He hastily wiped them with his shirt-sleeve and tried to compose himself. He looked straight ahead and did not say a word. He could feel the older woman's eyes on him. "What is your name?" she asked softly. When he did not respond, she tried again. "Where are your parents?"

He told her in a slow and steady voice that he did not know who or where his father was, but his mother was in another town. He did not want to give her too much information. He was scared and confused. He did not understand why this woman was choosing to show him kindness. He questioned her motivation, but he was compelled to tell her something about himself, at least to show her that he was not a bad person. He was not a thief. He was just a young boy who was struggling to reach a certain goal and was taking all the opportunities that were being thrown his way. Although common sense told him that this was one opportunity that he should have missed.

He told her his story. He had run away from home, not because he was maltreated, but because he could not stand the misery. They were poor. His mother had had way too many children by too many men, who would abandon her the moment she became pregnant. She had never learned her lesson and always hoped that the next one would be the savior. They never had enough to eat. The one person who always looked out for him to a certain extent had been his grandmother. She had an old, worn-out Yoruba Bible, and she would always recite the Psalms to him and his siblings in Yoruba.

He was his mother's first son, so he went to school whenever his mother could afford it, which meant not very often. He taught himself to read and write; whenever he saw books, his heart soared. He wanted to be something, but he felt stifled and restricted. This went on for years. There was never any consistency in his life. His mother was a pariah in the the town they lived in because of her numerous liaisons, so most people would rather gossip about her than try to help her. One day his grandmother fell ill and never recovered. Her death dealt him a heavy blow. It was shortly after that that a young girl came to the house. She was younger than him, and his mother introduced her as his younger sister.

She looked so clean.

When she sat in their house, he was scared that the dirt and grime would cling to her. She did not seem to notice any of that. Their mother was not really happy to see her. She received the presents that she brought reluctantly and did not ask any questions, leaving the two of them to talk.

She lived in Lagos with her father. He asked her questions about it, and she made it sound so beautiful. When she left, he longed to go with her, and as her visits became more frequent, it strengthened his resolve to leave the misery that he lived in and go in search of his destiny.

And one day he did. It was not like he had given it much thought. He just left, on a ride at the back of a truck headed to Lagos.

When he finished speaking, the older woman asked him for his age. She cringed when he told her.

"Why don't you try and look for your sister?" she asked.

He had thought of it several times but then he decided against it. His sister was living with her father. The last thing he wanted was to be a burden to anyone. His fierce sense of pride cautioned against it.

The older woman listened to his excuse and let out a loud sigh. "Listen to me, my son. This life that you have chosen is not the best."

She paused. "Do you know what they do to thieves when they get caught?"

He nodded his response.

At that moment they heard footsteps, and she whispered hastily, "Go and look for your sister. Get out of this life as soon as you can." She squeezed his hand and returned to the floor in the original position that he had found her.

Aloy appeared, and he knew it was time for them to swap places. He took the stairs by the twos to the top-floor apartment. The others were waiting for him. He did not go past the front door and was handed two bags. He knew what to do next. As he walked past the door of the bottom-floor apartment, he caught a glimpse of a sticker on the front door: *His Banner Over Us Is Love.* A feeling of warmth that he could not explain came over him. He was tempted to go back into the apartment, but that was not the plan. Instead he took the bags and walked as fast as he could to the designated meeting point.

Two hours later when the gang of thieves met, he was given his share of the loot. It was more money than he knew what to do with. As he and Aloy left, the latter had a newly acquired spring in his step.

He remained silent.

"*Wetin dey do you now?*" ("What is wrong with you? "), his companion spat at him. "*You just dey do like person wey don lose im mama, you no hear de tin wey Ol' Boi talk—im sey mission accomplished! So why you dey slack now?* "("What's wrong with you?" "You are acting like someone who has lost his mother. You heard what Ol' Boi said—mission accomplished! Why are you slacking? "). He did not answer. When they got to the bus stop, he made as if to catch the same bus as Aloy but let the older boy jump on, and he walked away.

Night had fallen by the time he got back to Aguda. The whole place was abuzz. Everyone was out rejoicing because the Nigerian team had won the match. He wanted to make his way to the room unnoticed when he heard Tonye's voice.

"Did you see the goal?" he said excitedly. "Where were you—?" He stopped when he saw the look on his friend's face.

"What happened to you?" he asked concernedly.

"I have to leave this place," was his curt response.

"This night?"

He shook his head. "Soon."

Tonye sighed. "*Where you dey go?*" ("Where are you going?")

"I have family," he said.

Tonye gazed at him, his eyes shining with surprise in the night light. He thought for a moment and then he said cynically, "*Look, na Lagos, we bin dey...nobody dey find anybody here o, if you know sey you get family, where dem dey when you dey do **asunta**?*" ("Look, this is Lagos! Nobody looks for anybody here. If you really had family here, where were they when you were sleeping outside?")

He did not know how to answer the question, so he kept quiet. His share of the loot was burning a hole of shame in the pocket of his trousers. The next day he found an old tin of Bournvita, and when he knew no one was looking, he hid the money inside and put the tin in the bag he carried around.

He went back to his normal routine as if nothing had changed. But he knew that he needed to make some changes, or at least try to.

It took him a week to decide what to do.

One Tuesday afternoon when Uncle sent him to the bank, he took his share of the loot from the tin and added it to the money to deposit. He did not want to spend any of the ill-gotten wealth. When he left the bank, he did not go back to the market. He went to the taxi park.

He found the house easily. It was on the corner of the street. A gray gate barricaded the compound. Looking around, he realized that the neighborhood was familiar. It was not far from here that he had committed his crime. He hesitated. What if someone recognized him? How would he explain that he had made a mistake? He decided that there was no going back now. He had nothing to lose. With a deep sigh, he peeped through the crack of the gate. He could see a man who looked like he was in his sixties seated on a chair, reading a newspaper. He knocked on the gate.

The man looked up from the paper and demanded, "Who is it?"

He did not know what to say, so he said his name. He could hear the man standing up and coming toward the gate. He knew the name meant nothing to him, so when the man got closer, he said his sister's name. "I am her brother," he added.

The man opened the gate and sized him up. He gestured for him to come in. There were voices coming from inside the house, mostly laughing female voices.

The man who had opened the gate for him sat down on the chair and asked him to sit in the other chair.

The man did not ask him anything, so he did not wait to be asked. He started to tell his story. He did not leave anything out. The man's face remained expressionless as he listened. When he finished talking, he was gasping for breath; it was a mixture of fear and uncertainty that overwhelmed him.

"What did you say your name is again?" the older man asked in a calm voice.

When he told him, he simply nodded, stood up, and went into the house. He began to get a bit scared. Maybe it was time to leave. He had said too much; maybe this had not been a good idea in the first place.

When the man returned, he was not alone. He was accompanied by the most beautiful woman he had ever seen. She must have been in her midfifties the way she carried herself, but she could have passed for much younger. She handed him a glass of water. He stood up and took it from her and thanked her as he drained the contents in seconds.

The woman was visibly amused. "Have you been running a race?" she asked, laughing.

The older man, who was folding his newspaper, responded in a matter-of-fact tone as he sat down. "Yes, he has. It's just that he's been running in the wrong direction."

The woman took the empty glass from him, let out a small laugh, and returned to the house.

"Sit down, Reuben," the older man said. "I am sure Enitanwa will be very happy to see you when she comes back."

The Fire Starter

*Y*ou had been having a particularly terrible day; the chap who owed you money had promised to pay you back that morning. You had arrived at his place, hoping to leave with the cash, but had been told that he had not been seen for the last four days. You knew where you could catch up with him, but still the inconvenience was more than you needed. You are walking away to the other side of the motor park, past the taxi park; a taxi is about to exit the park, and it slows down to allow the pedestrians to pass. You walk briskly and for some reason are compelled to turn and look at the occupant of the taxicab. Your eyes meet hers, and for the second time in the space of a few minutes, your stomach churns with the bitter juices of indignation. She has her right foot on her lap as she is seated in the back seat of the car. For that fleeting moment, you experience a mixture of feelings you can't begin to describe. The rays of the morning sun pierce through your hairless scalp. You cannot explain what you are feeling. It is almost like you are grieving for something you lost but never really had. You hasten your pace as you realize that you cannot predict what she could do to you now that she has seen you. Although you have prepared yourself for this inevitable encounter, it still manages to knock you off your already uneasy balance. The taxicab edges onto the busy road and speeds off. You watch it disappear into the horizon as you walk toward the noise of the bus conductors calling out various destinations in Lagos.

You have not thought about her for a long time; the sight of her leads to the eruption of indescribable emotions in you. Perhaps that is why you find yourself in the neighborhood where you had first met her. You are not sure exactly what you are expecting to accomplish when you wander into that corner of Yaba, but nothing prepares you for what life throws your way.

At first you think you are mistaken, but then you realize it is him. He has changed so much. He looks slightly older, and his clothes are clean, almost sparkling. You cross the road that separates you and walk toward him. Your face is pulled into a smile of pleasant astonishment. You halt as you realize that he is not alone. You realize that there is an older man with him. You want to establish a connection between the two of them, especially as you see them chatting amicably, almost like father and son.

Jealousy eats into you like maggots on the rotting carcass of a dead animal.

As the pair walk away, you follow several yards behind them. You instinctively realize that you don't want to be seen, and when he throws a glance over his shoulder, you swiftly duck and hide in a corner near the wall of the house, where you startle a gangly man who is calmly responding to the call of nature. You ignore the startled look on the man's face; you ignore the tirade of insults that he throws at you for daring to disrupt his moment of peace; you ignore the steady stream of liquid forming a triangulated pattern against the wall. You keep your eye on the pair, who by now has arrived at their destination, a quaint-looking house on the corner of a street. The house is barricaded by a gray gate.

The sign in front of the house says *Terra-Cotta Beauty*.

This means nothing to you, and you entertain a number of thoughts as you gesture to one of the numerous motorbikes that have been ambling up and down the slightly busy street.

You are still puzzled as you hop on the motorbike and tell the driver your destination. As the wind blows in your face, you feel the bile rising up your throat and have a sudden urge to throw up. Instead you spit out the bitter saliva that has coated the inside of your mouth. In the rapid movement of the vehicle that you are on, the saliva splashes on your face and on the back of the shirt of the *okada* driver. He curses you out loud, and you are too weak under the weight of pent-up emotions to respond in a similar manner, so you manage a curt yet pleading, *"Abeg, no vex."* ("Please, don't be annoyed")

You spend the rest of the day thinking about him, as you often have since he disappeared. You had felt a connection with him and had secretly ordained him your sidekick, the one who had your back when things went awry. You feel betrayed as you realize that the connection that you felt was phony and gave you a false sense of security. You berate yourself, as this has gone against your principle of not having any emotional attachments to anyone you work with—and why would you think he was different? The image of the house with the gray gate comes to your mind as you nurse feelings of bewilderment and depression. The stability and the coziness it represents aggravates your already volatile temperament. You wonder if he lives in the house or is just visiting the older man.

The next day you return to the neighborhood. You start skulking around the area to watch the comings and goings in the house with the gray gate for a couple of days, enough time to establish the nature of the domestic situation. You resolve not to have an unruly confrontation with him. That will just complicate things. His luck has clearly changed, and it is important that you use this to your advantage the best way you possibly can.

On the third day, you approach him. You have rehearsed it so many times before, and you are satisfied with the way it works out. You know he is surprised to see you, and he covers this up by pretending not to know who you are. He is walking down the road with the pretty girl you have often seen him with while watching him for the last two days. You know that they take an evening stroll at this time each day, and you have prepared yourself for this. From a distance she looked fat, but now as you are closer to her you realize that she is actually pregnant. She looks too young to be with child, and you wonder if he is the father. That irks you even more. How does he get away with being so lucky? Nice house, pretty lady, most certainly pretty baby. How did he hit this jackpot? He was nothing when you knew him, and now he seems to have everything you wish you had.

When he sees you, he tells her to walk ahead of him the short distance to the house with the gray gate. He remains silent as he watches her walk slowly toward the house; she turns briefly for a moment, and he gives her a reassuring nod. You also watch her and then turn to him. You are brimming with exuberance, and you share this with him as you ask him with a twinkle in your eye who the girl is. He does not respond to your question, and you ask again. He is looking around him, and then you realize that he is not proud to be seen in your company. You try to hide your feelings of despondency as you watch his eye movements.

"*Se, because your levels don change, you don forget your paddies?*" ("Is it because you are on a different level that you don't know your friends anymore?")

You are dealt a double blow when he replies in perfect English. "What exactly can I do for you?"

You are surprised by the question because you don't really know the answer. You don't know what you want him to do for you. You have not really thought about it. You just wanted to talk to him. He begins to walk away from you, and you pull him back. A slight shuffle ensues. You are taller and bigger, so you have the upper hand, and you hold both his hands tight. He seems a bit helpless, and your faces are inches apart; you can smell his breath and some strong, manly aftershave, nothing like anything you have ever used. You pull away from him. You are satisfied that you have managed to extract some reaction from him. His original melancholy attitude when he saw you irritated you. You tell him simply that you want money. Although that was not your original plan; you had just really wanted to satisfy your curiosity.

He tells you that he has no money for you, and that riles you even more. You threaten to expose him to the people that he is living with. He smiles sheepishly and tells you that they already know. He adds that, in spite of that, they welcomed him with open arms. You did not expect this, and you are searching in your mind for a worthy retort when he begins to walk away. You don't bother to stop him because you realize that you have no reason to.

You walk in the opposite direction. You feel so dejected. What did you do wrong? You feel like you have been in a boxing ring and your opponent has dealt you a thousand blows, leaving you too weak to retaliate. You end up in a beer parlor and drink bottle after bottle until the owner, a jovial lady, tells you that she is about to close up shop. You feel a cloud of happiness over you as you walk down the street. You congratulate yourself because no matter how many bottles of beer you end up drinking, you can never get drunk and are able to walk steadily out of the beer parlor.

You become so obsessed with him and his new life that you decide to come by the neighborhood as often as you can. Your stopping in front of the house with the *Terra-Cotta Beauty* sign depends on your mood. Sometimes you even think about her, and knowing what you did to her even though you had feelings for her makes your pilgrimage to the neighborhood somewhat cathartic. *Terra-Cotta Beauty*. You like the name, and by now you know enough about it to know that it is the central point of the neighborhood. A neighborhood you have known so well and done plenty of business in. You see him a couple of times, even though he never sees you, but you never try to approach him to ask him for money again.

One night you have had a little too much to drink, more than you usually do, and you are battling with a mixture of feelings. Perhaps it is the raw anger of knowing that someone has successfully moved out of this vile life you have been living that burns through you like a fiery raging bull. You want to do something about it. Let out some of the anger and frustration that has been building up inside you since the day you saw him. You look around you; someone has carelessly abandoned a kerosene lantern on the bench in front of the house next door. You pick it up and look straight into the dancing flame. You raise it up like a trophy and hurl it over the gate.

The Sacred Geometry of Chance

When they had first met, the girls had realized that they were close enough in age that there was really no delineation of authority. Adesuwa, the youngest, was always the one the other two thought to look out for. Mercy, the oldest, was the one the other two looked up to because she seemed to be ahead of them in the curve of life. It was something that would continue even after they became adults. Nneka was the middle one and a little bit of an enigma. Life ended up being a little harder for her than the other two, but it did not make her less self-assured.

Mercy was the only one of them who did not live with her parents when they met. They were in awe of this, but for Mercy, the youngest child of her parents, born in the twilight of their years, the fact that she had had to live with one older sibling or relative from the moment she turned five was not something that she had really enjoyed. She had yearned for the sort of familiar stability that the other two girls had had, and for a long time, she felt that she did not really belong anywhere.

She had lived first with her older brother and his family, and then she had moved in to stay with an aunt—her mother's younger sister. It was a domestic situation that had not ended well—the aunt was persnickety and paid attention to details that often did not make sense or even matter, and she seemed oblivious to the fact that her children were rude and unruly and her husband had an inability to function without consuming an alcoholic beverage. Mercy, the one who technically did not belong in the core family, was always the victim of the abuse and the beatings. That ordeal created in her a tendency to navigate through life with a somewhat stoic resilience, determined to be able to make something out of herself but not too fazed by the whims and fancies of human beings.

When her older sister, Lilian, had invited her to come and stay with her just before the arrival of her first child, Mercy had accepted more out of curiosity than anything else. She and Lilian had never had an opportunity to get close, as the latter had been in boarding school when Mercy was born, and they had never actually lived under the same roof. It was an opportunity for her to get to know her older sibling, but rather than strengthen their relationship, the first few months threatened to tear them apart.

The combination of a number of factors culminated in the cold war that erupted between the two sisters. Bade, Lilian's husband, was becoming more and more involved in political activism, something that made his wife extremely nervous and easily agitated. The other thing was that Lilian was more than a little bit disappointed in her sister's choice of profession. Lilian saw a younger version of herself in her sister, and, in mapping out her future for her, she had taken it upon herself to get the entrance forms for the same teacher training college that she had attended. The forms were pretty hard to come by, and she had used her clout as an alumna to get them. She had not consulted Mercy first and had presumptively assumed that her sister would want to become a teacher. When she had learned about this, Mercy had balked. She did not see herself as a teacher. She had neither the patience nor the aptitude that the teaching profession required. Without telling her sister, she applied and was accepted into the Institute of Fashion Design. When the stories fell into place, the battle line had been drawn. Lilian took her sister's decision to go to fashion school as an act of defiance, and from then on, there was nothing that Mercy did that could please her. She convinced herself that Mercy had some sordid hidden agenda.

It was Bade's mother who had intervened in the cold war between the sisters. She had seen Lilian's initial excitement upon her sister's arrival dissipate into a cold form of resentment and realized that this was quite unusual. Her first intervention had failed. Lilian was too stubborn and somewhat territorial—this was her sister, and Bade's mother had no right to intervene in **her** family business. Somewhat amused, the older woman had decided that the best thing was for the two of them to be away from each other as frequently as possible to give Lilian's frayed nerves a chance to heal. Neither of them argued against this. The sight of her sister irritated Lilian, and Mercy, on the other hand, was keen to broaden her social landscape.

This was how she had met Nneka and Adesuwa. Not realizing that these two would play a key role in the story of her life, Mercy had accompanied Mrs. Omotosho to the salon where she got her hair done. Adesuwa's mom, who owned the salon, seeing that Mercy was close in age to her own daughter, had summoned Adesuwa to come down and keep Mercy company. Ordinarily Adesuwa would have tried her best to be as caustic as she could. She had long grown out of her mother's playdate arrangements, but there was something about Mercy that spoke to her. Perhaps it was Mercy's nonchalant approach to life. They started to talk, and it was not long before Nneka showed up. Nneka lived three streets away from Adesuwa. Her father ran the household with ironclad rules, and although Nneka and Adesuwa knew each other, they hardly saw each other because the latter was not allowed to socialize much. On that day she had come to deliver something that Adesuwa's mother had ordered from their family shop. The three girls started chatting, and when the time came for Nneka to leave, they had walked her back to her house. So a friendship developed. Although the threesome did not see each other that often, there was never any shortage of things to talk about when they did. With time they grew closer and stayed in step with each other. Although they all came from different backgrounds and had different personalities, they had a sort of indescribable bond that would seal them together for a long time.

Although Adesuwa lived in a house that had constant traffic and was always surrounded by people, deep inside she felt very lonely. This gave people who did not know her well the impression that she was an introvert. The truth was that while she was really unimpressed by the ebb and flow of people that came through her mother's salon over the years, she was secretly on a mission to meet the one person who would make her weak at the knees, create butterflies in her stomach, sweep her off her feet, whisper sweet nothings into her ear, and carry her away into the sunset while they made a dozen babies together. She had come to this realization, (after reading one too many romance novels), by the time she had turned fourteen. It was an epiphany that had been waiting for the perfect moment to reveal itself, and from that moment, she knew that her life would be meaningless unless she found him. Granted, she had no idea who he was, but she would be ready when she found him, and it would all be perfect.

Nneka, on the other hand, thought her life was totally meaning-less. It lacked any form, shape, or purpose except that which had been endorsed by her father—the almighty Benedict Uchendu. Her duties consisted of making sure she received excellent grades in school and helping her mother out in the family shop that was adjacent to the house. The family had a reputation for not being too friendly. This was mostly thanks to the patriarch of the family who forbade any form of socializing

Nneoma, Nneka's sister and only sibling, was four years younger. When they were much younger, Nneoma had secretly revealed to Nneka that she had a strong desire to serve God in an unmarried state by becoming a nun. According to her this was the only state in which she could truly serve him, free from all the encumbrances of the flesh and its accompanying carnal nature. Upon hearing that Nneka realized that she and her sister were truly opposites, like par-allel lines that could never meet.

The one thing that added a slight spark to her life was that dur-ing the Christmas holidays, the family drove to their father's home-town in the eastern part of the country. Their father was one of six siblings and the only one who lived in Lagos; for that reason he and his family were treated like royalty whenever they arrived at the family homestead. Left to their own whims and fancies, Nneka was always happy to regale her cousins with stories of Lagos, stories that were a huge departure from her actual reality. Tales were spun of parties she imagined she had attended, friends she wished she had made, places she longed to visit. Nneoma, the quieter of the two girls, was content to play the silent observer as her sister transported her cousins into a world that existed only in her mind. But Nneka was confident that one day she would break loose. Unlike Adesuwa she did not have any fancy or romanticized notions; she just knew that anything was better than being constantly stuck under someone's thumb. The irony was that for both girls, it would take almost the same set of circumstances to change their lives.

Adesuwa and Nneka took the university entrance examinations at the same time. Adesuwa failed at her first try and was unable to get into the university to study anything tangible. Her parents decided that she needed to work harder and sent her to a highly rated remedial school so that she could get the personal tutoring she needed to take the exams again. Nneka's university entrance examination results had fallen a mere thirty points short of the required cutoff for entrance into the college of medicine at the University of Lagos. She was, however, accepted to study biology at the same university, much to the chagrin of her father, who had always wanted her to be a medical doctor. According to Mercy, if the right amount of money had changed hands, Nneka would be studying medicine. But Benedict Uchendu was too regimented to believe in bribery.

He had a different plan in mind. He was convinced that if she studied hard and got excellent grades in her course of study, she could write a letter to the board of governors of the university and request a transfer to medical school. However, the truth was that Nneka did not want to study biology or medicine. If anyone had asked her, and unfortunately no one did, she would have said that she wanted to do exactly what Mercy was doing. She wanted to make clothes. For years she had been making clothes for the family on her mother's sewing machine, and she had become quite good. It had been a consequence of an edict passed on by her father, who, realizing that money could be saved, had declared that the family would do better to buy fabric and sew their clothes themselves. It also helped that one of his brothers sold fabric for a living, so they got most of their clothes practically for free. But heaven forbid that she let her father know that she wanted to make a profession out of it. As far as he was concerned, this was something that other people's children did. His children became doctors and lawyers.

A single encounter with a stranger can change one's life, making your destiny take an unexpected twist. For Nneka, it happened one afternoon. She was alone in the shop, studying for an upcoming test in anatomy. Her mother was out running errands, and the street was unusually quiet. Very few people had stopped by, and then he appeared, seemingly from nowhere. He had that appearance that boys have when they are on the verge of manhood: a sprinkling of facial hair, the telltale signs of an emerging beard and mustache. When he spoke, she could tell that it had not been long since his voice had broken, and he added to the baritone with an artificial gruffness. He looked at her intently and asked for a box of cigarettes. She handed it to him and collected the money, more than the price of the cigarettes, and she rummaged through the money box for the correct amount of change.

"How much are those biscuits?" he asked, pointing to a packet of HobNobs, which happened to be her favorite. She told him the price, and as she made to hand it to him, he raised his hand and said, "No, my dear. That's for you." She was still trying to recover from that when he declared, "Keep the change."

She looked at him, slightly bewildered, and he winked at her and smiled. It was not the first time that someone had bought something from the shop for her. When it did happen, it was someone that she knew—one of the neighbors, a friend who decided that she needed a treat. It was also not the first time that she had been winked at—sometimes the boys from her class would try to get cozy because they wanted her to give them something they could not have, but they had known her long enough to understand now that she was the ultimate prude. She tried to understand why this total stranger would show her this kindness for no reason. She was quite certain that she had never seen him before, and lest she forget her manners, she whispered, "Thank you," to which he responded, "Anything for you, your majesty." That succeeded in throwing her off guard again.

She was still trying to recover from that when she realized that he had disappeared, just as furtively as he had appeared. She looked around the corner, but he was nowhere to be seen. The only thing that proved that he was not a figment of her imagination was the money in her hands and the cigarette smell that hung in the air. She wondered if she would ever see him again and secretly hoped that she would. Everything about him screamed that she should run fast in the opposite direction, but there was something about the way he'd said "your majesty" that made her want to hear him say it again.

From that day she began to think about what she would say to him the next time she saw him, how she would act: certainly less coy, less naïve, savvier, more confident. She longed to tell her friends about him, but something in her told her to keep it a secret. He came from a different social class than they did, and she was too ashamed to even let anyone know that she was associating herself with someone of that nature.

He showed up again about a week later. This time Nneoma was in the shop with her.

"Hello, your majesty," he said, so smoothly that she bristled. Nneoma scowled at him.

Ignoring her, Nneka offered her widest smile. "Shall I get you your usual?" she asked flippantly, pretending that this was not just the second time that she had seen him and that thoughts of him had not preoccupied her mind for the last week. He nodded, and she continued by asking, "What is your name?"

His English was a little broken, but she tried to ignore that as he said, "My name is Aloy, Madam Nneka." She was about to ask him how he knew her name when they were interrupted by Nneoma, who blurted out the price of the cigarettes and announced that they did not have any change.

He glanced at the younger girl and handed the money over to her. "Keep the change," he said smoothly. Nneka gave her sister a scathing look while the latter, still scowling, took a seat on the only chair in the small shop.

They made small talk before he left. She could not even remember what they talked about, and when she turned to look at her sister, she was still frowning.

"I don't like that boy," Nneoma announced to no one in particular.

Nneka looked at her sister, arms akimbo. "First of all, that is not a boy; that is a man." She pointed in the direction that Aloy had gone. "Second of all, you do not even know him, so how can you even like him or not?" She said this rolling her eyes and throwing her hands in the air.

"Well, you like him," Nneoma said boldly.

"Well, I know him," Nneka responded.

"Where do you know him from?"

"None of your business," she said and then added, "He is a friend from school."

"Why does he even have to call you your majesty?" she said, mimicking Aloy's voice. When her sister did not answer, she repeated what she had said before, this time with greater emphasis. "I don't like him."

Nneka continued to ignore her. She could not believe that he had actually come back. She was already daydreaming about the next time she would see him.

The next time she saw him, she was on her way back from afternoon classes and had just gotten off the bus. He seemed to come out of nowhere and walked her toward the house. They walked slowly, talking about everything and anything, but parted ways before they got closer to her house. Her mother would be at the shop, and the last thing she needed was to be asked questions that even she did not know the answers to. She had no way of knowing what she was doing or what she was feeling. Was this love? Or was it just a mere infatuation? Common sense told her it was the latter.

Aloy brought with him the energy from another world. It was an energy that she could never have experienced in her simple and parochial life.

The next time Mercy came over to the neighborhood, she came to the shop to see Nneka.

"You that you never come and see somebody?" Mercy accused her friend.

Nneka smiled. "You know how it is, with school—"

Mercy raised her hand in the air to silence her friend. "That is no excuse, my dear friend...I go to school too, you know," Mercy said with a hint of despondency. "I am just coming from Adesuwa's," she continued. "Her mom said she is still in school, and I said I would go and see her there. Come with me."

Nneka hesitated. She knew that this was something that she was not allowed to do but did not know how she would tell her friend.

Mercy interpreted her friend's hesitation for something else and suggested, "If you are worried about the shop, Nneoma is here, and she can stay here, right?"

Nneoma had been silent the whole time and now looked up from the book she was reading. She did not say anything but looked at her sister as if to tell her that she already knew the answer to this question. But Nneka was determined to do something different. She was tired of following rules that did not make sense to her.

Her face lit up as she announced, "Of course, let's go. Which bus are we taking?"

She ignored the horrified look on her younger sister's face as she accompanied Mercy down the road toward the bus stop. It had been a while since they had done anything together, and she needed this little adventure. On the bus ride to Adesuwa's school, she quizzed Mercy about her school. What was it like? How many classes did she need to take? How did they do the sketches? Mercy answered her friend's questions as graciously as she could. She knew that Nneka harbored an instinctive desire to make clothes and had even seen some of her sketches, which were better than anything she could do, but she was too coy to let her know that.

By the time they arrived at Adesuwa's school, it was closing time. They searched the throng of people pouring out of the gate for Adesuwa, but it was she who saw them first. Screaming with delight, she held her friends in a warm embrace, and the contents of her handbag tumbled out. Laughing, all three girls bent down to gather the runaway items; others scrambled to help them.

One of them was a young boy who handed Adesuwa her notepad. He reminded Nneka of Aloy, but he seemed a little more polished and less uncouth. He and Adesuwa exchanged a look, and Adesuwa felt something in her stomach. Could he be the one that she had been dreaming of? He seemed so unassuming, so ordinary. He walked away without saying anything, but the exchange had not gone unnoticed by her friends, who would tease her on the bus ride back.

"I wonder what his name is," said Nneka dreamily.

"Have you seen him before?" asked Mercy.

Giggling, Adesuwa shook her head.

They spent the rest of the ride home making up names for Adesuwa's new "friend" and pairing the make-believe last names with Adesuwa, erupting with laughter when Nneka came up with Mrs. Adesuwa Charming.

Adesuwa looked forward to seeing this boy again and finding out what exactly that look meant.

Nneka continued her routine with Aloy. He would meet her at the bus stop as she came home from school, and they would walk to a safe distance from her house before they parted ways. He was funny and quick-witted, the sort of boy who would make a girl believe that he could bring her the moon and the stars, and even though she knew it was not true, she could not be bothered with the truth, as she enjoyed the way it made her feel. She tried to get him to tell her a little bit of himself but always sensed a reluctance to do so, and she did not push further. She was enjoying her secret escapade, and although part of her did not want to jeopardize it, most of her—the part that was sensible—was screaming for someone to see them together and question his motives. She needed something to jolt her back to reality

Looking back, she could have sensed something was amiss, especially when he would ask about the people who lived in the neighborhood. Burglaries were not strange and were now becoming more common, but still, it was shortly after she had told Aloy that Mrs. Labinjo had just returned from the United Kingdom, where she had visited her daughter who was studying there, that their house had been burgled. She had heard from someone that Mr. Adams engaged in trade transactions, which meant that he had to bring large sums of money home over the weekend when the banks were closed. She had told Aloy this, and the Adams family was robbed the weekend. Yet none of this added up until the Mama Kenneth incident.

Mama Kenneth was their neighbor, four houses down. She was a nurse and worked the nightshift. Her husband worked in Cameroon and only came home for Easter and Christmas holidays. They had three sons who, although they were teenagers, led independent lives and were wont to stay with relatives nearby. But on occasion they would come home unannounced, quite often when their mother was away at work. It was for this reason that Mama Kenneth often left the keys to her house with the Uchendus.

Nneka and Aloy were at the shop when Mama Kenneth came over that evening. She was off to work and knew that her eldest son might decide to come home since he was getting ready for exams and preferred the solitude of the house to study. Nneka took the keys from her; it was a routine that had been ongoing for years, and no further explanation was needed.

As she left, Aloy asked, "How often does she do that?"

Nneka was distracted, reading a magazine that Aloy had brought for her. She wanted to go through it before he left, because even though he had said it was a gift, she knew that fashion magazines like that were not allowed in her house.

"Do what?" she asked without looking up.

"Leave her keys with you."

"I don't know; you heard what she said about her son, and she is not coming back until tomorrow." She looked up then. "Why do you want to know?"

"No reason," he shrugged. "I was just curious."

Someone came to the shop, and when she finished attending to that person, she was disappointed to see that Aloy had left without saying good-bye. It was at that moment that she noticed that the keys to Mama Kenneth's house were not on the counter where she had placed them. She looked all over the place for them; perhaps they had fallen to floor. She had spent several minutes looking for them when it dawned on her that there was only one thing that could have happened. Aloy must have taken them. Her heart beat faster as she wondered what he would want to do with the keys to someone else's house. She was still trying to come up with a possible reason for him to take the keys to Mama Kenneth's house when Nneoma appeared.

"Watch the shop; I am coming," she said. She walked briskly down the street, ignoring Nneoma's protests that it was not her turn to stay at the shop and she had merely come to keep her company.

Nneka's heart was pounding as she approached Mama Kenneth's house. She prayed that her intuition was wrong and that Aloy was nowhere near Mama Kenneth's house and had left to go home, wherever home was. Night was beginning to fall, and she was a little scared, but she was determined to satisfy her conscience.

The front door to the house was shut. She turned the door handle, and sure enough it opened. Aloy stood there stuffing his pocket with a mass of shiny gold. He had not heard her come in, and her loud gasp alerted him to her presence. He smiled. It was the widest smile that she had seen him smile, and then he tried to hold her hand. She backed away.

"You are a thief," she blurted out, more as a confirmation to herself. There was a sour taste forming in her mouth, and she felt that she was going to throw up. She had never felt so betrayed in her life, and what he said next would only confirm that betrayal.

"Nneka, I really like you." He was still smiling, albeit a little awkwardly.

"You are a thief." She repeated it not just because she knew that it was true, but also because she had to let him know the difference between them.

How could someone be so vile? She felt an anger forming inside her, an anger that was directed more at herself than him. How could she have been so senselessly stupid? Of all the voices that echoed in her head, it was her sister's voice that was the loudest: "*I don't like that boy.*" Oh, if only she had seen then what Nneoma in her wisdom had seen, she would have no reason to be standing here confronting this malapert rogue. She knew she had to act fast. It would be very hard to explain what they were both doing here at this time.

She stretched her hand out and said softly, "Give me what you have taken."

He must have been taken aback by her audacity, because although he hesitated, he put his hand in his pocket and handed his bounty to her. She gestured to him again, and he gave her the keys.

Satisfied, she said very slowly and calmly, "You have to leave now."

She felt herself starting to shake and was more fearful that she would show any sign of weakness in front of him. She did not want to give him that satisfaction. Later, much later, she would cry and mourn the loss of her innocence.

He turned to look at her one more time before he left but did not say anything.

She had been in Mama Kenneth's house once before but never upstairs. Holding on to the gold trinkets, she made her way up. It was now dark, and she opened the door of one of the bedrooms. It made a squeaky noise that irritated her, but she ignored it as she entered in. She was lucky; it was the master bedroom. All she had to do was put the gold on the nearest surface and leave.

The lights came on in the room within seconds of her entering in. She squinted as she adjusted her sight. It had been several months since she had seen Mama Kenneth's husband, and she almost mistook him for an intruder, one of Aloy's accomplices. They were both shocked, and when he saw what she held in her hands, the shock on his face was transformed into anger.

"If you were a man, I would beat the living daylights out of you. You dare to come into my house and steal." His voice thundered through the house, and she knew that no amount of explanation was possible to cover up for what he had seen with his own eyes.

Even when she was back at her house, in front of her parents, with accusing fingers pointing at her, she could not find the words. Papa Kenneth explained that he had returned home from Cameroon that afternoon and had taken a long nap. He had heard noises but had remained silent and calm, hoping to surprise the burglars when the time was right. He had caught Nneka in his bedroom with his wife's eighteen-carat gold necklaces in her hand.

Nneka's pleas of her innocence fell on deaf ears as Papa Kenneth declared, "Only God knows what else she would have taken if I had not caught her." It was the ultimate disgrace as they stood in the living room of her parent's house. Her father had remained silent throughout the time the story was narrated. He now cleared his throat and politely asked if anything else was missing from Papa Kenneth's house beyond the items that had been found with Nneka.

Papa Kenneth shifted from one side to the other and hesitated before saying, "I will have to check o!"

Benedict Uchendu suggested, "Why don't you check and please let me know." It was an easy way to be polite and rude at the same time. With that one sentence he had dismissed Papa Kenneth from his presence and his house. The younger man was led out by Nneka's mother, who whispered silent apologies interjected with self-ruminations of how they were expected to live down this shame.

In the silence of the living room, Nneka tried to think of a story that would not include any reference to Aloy but would nevertheless be convincing enough to explain her presence in a house she had no reason to be in. Later in life, whenever she thought about that night, she would always wonder why she had not been given an opportunity to provide some form of explanation. Her father sat looking straight ahead while her mother huddled in a corner. Nneka could tell she was sad and afraid, two emotions that a fragile and timid woman like her could not handle very well. The words that her husband spoke next could have broken Doris Uchendu, but rather there was a wave of relief—relief that the ordeal was not being prolonged more than needed.

"You will leave my house immediately." The last word was said with such firmness that it left Nneka at a loss for words. A light gasp came from the hallway leading to the bedrooms, revealing the hitherto furtive presence of Nneoma, who had been hiding in the shadows, taking it all in.

Numb, broken, and dejected, Nneka left the house. No words were spoken. It was not until she was in the darkness of the street that it actually dawned on her that she had nowhere to go. Where would she go to? How would she explain how she had come to be in the situation she was in? She wandered aimlessly down the street, thinking.

At one point she found herself in front of Mama Kenneth's house and hurried past, not wanting to linger at the scene of the crime, lest she be accused of something else. She did notice that the lights in the house were off. An indication that Papa Kenneth had probably gone back to sleep and had no intention of returning to her father.

The streets were unusually quiet that night. A few people walked briskly past her, but she kept her head down. She did not want to attract unnecessary attention. It was just a question of time before people found out about what had happened. How would she live it down? She had never been so ashamed in her life. The realization that she had nowhere to go was making things more painful than ever.

She looked up and saw the Terra-Cotta Beauty sign a short distance away. She had not seen Adesuwa since the day she had gone to see her at her school. She had been lucky that day, as she had returned just in time, before anyone had realized that she had gone somewhere without asking for permission. And look at her now. Roaming the streets like a homeless person. Until it jumps into hot water, a frog does not realize that there are two worlds.

She put her thoughts in motion. Adesuwa's parents had always been kind and accommodating. Perhaps if she went to them, they would find a way to talk to her father. She walked through the gate, which was hardly ever locked, and knocked on the front door and waited. There was a light on in the salon on the lower level—an indication that someone was awake. Another flood of shame rushed through her, and she secretly hoped that there was no late-night customer in the salon. She was already uncomfortable enough explaining her predicament to the Erhabors, let alone a complete stranger.

She knocked again, and this time she heard some movement. Mrs. Erhabor opened the door. She looked surprised, then anxious. To the

unasked question, Nneka started to say something by way of an explanation, but instead she burst out crying and lost herself completely,
sobbing uncontrollably.

Mrs. Erhabor led her into the house, and before long, the older
woman was hovering over her patiently, handing her a glass of water.
Nneka took light sips of the water and proceeded to narrate her story.
She left out the parts of Aloy, which would have been hard to tackle.

She tried to interpret the look on Mrs. Erhabor's face as she
ended her story. Had she made a mistake coming here? She was
already starting to contemplate her other options, which did not
extend beyond spending the night on the street, when Adesuwa's
mom spoke. "There is nothing that you have told me that cannot wait
until the morning. For now, since your parents are not happy with
you. I think it is best if you spent the night here." She stood up and
took the now empty glass from Nneka. "Go to Adesuwa's room. Good-
night, my dear," she said with a light smile. It was the best thing that
Nneka had heard all day.

When she got upstairs, she knocked lightly on Adesuwa's door and
went in without waiting for an answer. She was surprised to find that
her friend was still awake. Adesuwa was not surprised to see Nneka.
Her first thought was that her mother had sent for her to provide some
sort of moral support to her present dilemma.

"How now?" she said cheerily. She sat on the edge of the bed, and
as she looked closer, she noticed that Adesuwa had been crying.

Adesuwa did not wait to be asked before she said, "I am in big
trouble." Adesuwa patted a spot on the bed beside her, and Nneka
moved closer. "I am pregnant," she whispered. Even in the darkened
room, Adesuwa could see her friend's eyes widen.

"With what?" she whispered back.

"A baby, of course," she said with a light chuckle. This was the last
thing Nneka had expected to hear, and she realized that her situation
paled miserably compared to Adesuwa's. Yet Adesuwa was still at home
sleeping in her own bed despite the gravity of her offense.

"Do you remember that boy we saw in my school the other day?"

Nneka gasped. "Oh my goodness, what did he do to you?"

Adesuwa laughed and took her friend's hand. "Relax!" she said reassuringly. She let out another light chuckle. "In fact, if anyone did anything to anyone, I am the one who should be guilty."

Nneka gave her friend a puzzled look. She found it amazing that she could retain her sense of humor at a time like this and listened as Adesuwa told her story.

The day after they had exchanged the look, Adesuwa had searched purposefully for him. His name was Afolabi Durosimi. She was surprised that she had not noticed him before, but he clearly had seen her several times because not only did he know her name, he also knew what classes she was taking. She would have liked to have called the look that they exchanged "love at first sight," but that was not what it was; it was more like "curiosity at first sight" followed by a gradual discovery. It was nothing strong and heady like she had read about in the romance books she had devoured in a bid to get into this theory of love. One day he did not exist; the next day he did.

They started talking about everything and nothing, and then she realized that she liked him and enjoyed his company. It was a different kind of like—not anything that she felt for anyone else. It was his calm and reassuring demeanor that made her feel so special. She had been too ashamed to admit this to him until he had confessed that he really liked her. Their first and only sexual encounter had been her idea. It had been the first time for both of them, and she had done all the coercing. Once had been enough because now she was carrying their child.

As the story ended, Nneka felt lethargic. It was the ultimate climax that she needed to the fast-moving emotional roller coaster that she had been on throughout the day. She tried to compare Adesuwa's description of her first love to hers and knew instantly that it was incomparable. She and Aloy had used each other. She had used him to escape to the fantasy land that would take her away from her stymied existence. He had used her as a source of information as he burgled her neighborhood. Granted, his offense was a thousand times worse than hers, but she had known from the start that he was not good for her, but she had played along nevertheless because she needed the distraction. She longed to tell Adesuwa about Aloy, but she needed time to get over the overwhelming shame that she felt. Her friend did not ask any probing questions, and they both fell asleep, expectant about what the next day would bring.

The next day brought a grief-stricken Mercy with the news that Mrs. Omotosho had been hospitalized. It was a bleak day for all of them, mostly for Mercy, who had leaned on her sister's mother-in-law as her benefactor and mother figure. It was an unusual relationship but one that came at a time when Mercy needed it most, especially when her relationship with her sister had started to turn sour. Over the last few weeks, she had been so preoccupied as she prepared to wrap up her studies in fashion design that she had neglected to look after Bade's mom the way she should have, and that weighed heavily on her.

As her friends tried to reassure her that there was nothing she could have done, Mercy realized that a lot of things were going to change if Mrs. Omotosho did not get better—or worse, passed away. It was time for her to mentally prepare for this. How could she have missed this? The older woman had been shrinking right before their eyes, ever since her son had been imprisoned for the second time. The trumped-up charges of treason and conspiracy to overthrow the government were not only laughable; they were beyond comprehension. The knowledge of this did not lessen the agony, but there was some consolation that at least this time they knew where he was. Yet with each visit, his mother had been shrinking and becoming a shadow of herself.

It was possible that her condition was further aggravated by the nonchalant attitude of Bade's father. The sardonic Papa Omotosho showed no interest in his son's predicament and carried on with his regular routine as if there were no fires burning around him. It was when her husband's complete disregard of the reality they were faced with became too much for her to bear that Mrs. Omotosho moved in with Lilian and Mercy. The official reason was that she wanted to be closer to Lilian and help out when the baby arrived, but anyone who saw her knew that it would be a bad idea to entrust a newborn into her care. She was too weak and frail and would often drift away into the shadows, deep in thought and contemplation.

At first Mercy would convince Mrs. Omotosho to come with her to Terra-Cotta Beauty to have her hair done. It was interesting how time had reversed the roles. It was the same way that Mrs. Omotosho had convinced Mercy to accompany her to the salon when she had observed that all was not right between her and her sister. There was never a lack of conviviality in the salon. The colorful cast of characters who came and went made sure of that. Every so often, there would be a slight spark in Mrs. Omotosho's eyes, almost like she was back to herself again. When Bade's trial was over and he was sentenced to life in prison, his mother had refused to leave the house. Mrs. Erhabor would come to the house to do her friend's hair and try to bring back some joy. It was futile; this time it was clear that she was approaching the point of no return, and a solid intervention would be needed to help her bounce back.

Mercy had woken up at the crack of dawn that morning when she found Mrs. Omotosho's lifeless body lying languid at the back of the house. Lilian was still asleep, and knowing she had to act fast, she had called on the neighbors to help. One neighbor stayed in the house with Lilian and her young son. They had conspiratorially agreed that nothing would be said to Lilian and had conjured up some story of Mrs. Omotosho needing to go to see her husband and Mercy accompanying her. When they got to the hospital, they were thankful that she was still breathing, but that emotion was short-lived when the doctor announced that her vital signs were too weak for them to expect anything but the worst to follow. Mercy left the hospital and went straight to Terra-Cotta Beauty, where she shared the news with an already emotionally burdened Mrs. Erhabor. She narrated the story to her friends between tears and sobs.

"I don't know what I will do if this woman dies," she said.

Her friends were helpless in consoling her. Words were not sufficient. It was Mrs. Erhabor who swung into action, taking over the management of affairs. Mr. Erhabor broke the news to Papa Omotosho and drove him to the hospital to be with his wife. Mrs. Erhabor had asked one of her friends, a medical doctor, to accompany her to see Lilian—they had decided that it might be necessary to sedate Lilian as she was heavy with child, and it would be better to calm her nerves. Mrs. Erhabor also thought it would be a good idea for Lilian, Mercy, and the little boy to move in with her while all this was going on.

They were wrong on both accounts. Lilian refused to be sedated. She also refused to leave her home. Long-suffering, she had developed a stiff sort of resilience, as if she was ready for whatever direction the wind of life decided to blow at her from. Impressed by her courage and strength, Mrs. Erhabor left, giving Mercy strict instructions to keep her informed of all that happened.

Mrs. Omotosho did not linger too long. She stayed in the hospital for a couple of days and passed away peacefully in her sleep on the evening of the second day.

Deep in mourning, they welcomed Lilian and Bade's daughter. It was quickly followed by the realization that Lilian could no longer afford to keep the house they had been living in. It would be more cost-effective and possibly safer for her and her sister to move in with Mr. Omotosho. It would be better, so they could somehow console them-selves. Those who suggested the latter did not know Mr. Omotosho. Lilian only agreed because she saw the practical aspect of it. Her father-in-law lived in a compound with two duplexes. He and his wife had lived in one, and for years they had had a series of tenants renting the second one. The latest set of tenants had just vacated the second duplex, and he offered to have Lilian live in there for a much-reduced rent. It was certainly out of the question for her to live there for free. Mercy dreaded the prospect of this. She was almost done with her studies and would soon be able to establish her independence. Under normal circumstances she would have moved into a place of her own, but under the present situation, it was totally out of the question. She knew Mr. Omotosho by reputation and had witnessed his laid-back attitude to a very severe family problem. Even though their interaction with Mr. Omotosho would be seemingly minimal—they would be liv-ing in separate houses—the last thing she wanted to do was leave her sister, nephew, and niece with the most emotionally selfish person she had ever had the misfortune to encounter. She knew she had made the right decision the day they arrived.

On moving day, there was a lot to do and pack. They had borrowed a friend's car, which Lilian was driving. By the time they arrived at Mr. Omotosho's, the gates to the compound were locked from the inside. A message had been left indicating that the gates were always locked at seven o'clock at night as a security precaution, and anyone who was not in the compound at that time would have to make alternative arrangements to spend the night. This message was delivered by a sympathetic neighbor, who, seeing their desolate plight, invited the foursome to spend the night in her living room.

While her sister seethed with rage, Lilian silently prayed for an opportunity to return this gesture to Papa Omotosho. As long as they lived together in that compound, she would get her vengeance on the dour, dull-faced man who opened the gates to let them in the next morning shortly after the crack of dawn. Who did not know that the traffic in Lagos could keep people out of their homes well beyond the seven o'clock hour? Unless the old man planned to remain a hermit in the house, she knew she would pay him back.

Nneka came to live with them about two months after they moved in. For Mercy it was a huge relief to have her friend in the house with her. Lilian was prone to long moments of deep reflection and solitude, something that Mercy could understand but not relate to. Besides, there was only so much company that she could get from an infant and a toddler, no matter how adorable they were. She had longed for some youthful adult company that was devoid of sadness and moodiness. By this time Nneka's complicated domestic situation was common knowledge, and Mercy resisted probing her to find out what exactly had happened. The important thing was to move on. There was already enough sadness and gloom in the household anyway.

It was even more energizing to learn that Nneka was ready to put her long-dormant design skills to use. It also helped that they were on the same creative wavelength. Together they could create some of the most outstanding pieces imaginable. Often working through the night, they set about creating their own fashion label: *Ariya Couture.* It was a name that was totally devoid of anything either of them represented. *Ariya* was the Yoruba word for *party,* and neither of them had a bustling social life to speak of, but since it was a women's clothing line and the word had a "feel-good' factor that meant that the ladies who wore their clothes would feel their best. It felt right.

It took a lot of intense hard work and often sleepless nights for them to accomplish what they needed to do. They wanted to first make a ready-to-wear collection before they opened up to made-to-order clothes. They converted a room in the house into their workroom and used Nneka's designs, which were stunning, and got a secondhand sewing machine that still had a lot of life left in it. They used the local *ankara* fabric, which they embellished with gems and sequins to produce styles never before seen.

A very pregnant Adesuwa became their muse. She was often accompanied by Reuben, who had recently showed up and settled into the Terra-Cotta Beauty household. He was also one of the most dependable people that the girls had ever met. He was quick to get them supplies (sewing thread, machine oil) at the drop of a hat. When the time came for them to launch their collection, he would be instrumental in delivering their flyers to parts of Lagos that they did not know existed, judging from the places some of their customers said they had traveled from.

They had decided early on, that to simplify things it would be easier for them to work out of the house. Lilian had balked at this notion at first, declaring that Papa might not approve of this, until the younger girls had reminded her that the advantage of their separate living quarters was that he did not need to know what was going on in their space as long as they did not bother him. Besides, they needed the additional income. Needless to say, it did not stop him from casting suspicious glances at any of their customers that he encountered in the compound, and of course he never responded to any of their greetings, which meant that a lot of people mistook him for a deaf old man.

Ariya Couture's first customers were Uloma and Olawunmi. On their first encounter, they would regale Nneka and Mercy with their tales of commuting to work by taking public transportation in the city of Lagos, including a recent adventure that they had had on a ferry.

As Reuben became a more frequent visitor to the ladies of Ariya Couture, helping them with this and that, Papa Omotosho also took it upon himself to turn him into his own personal errand boy, something the younger boy welcomed, as he was always ready to help out, and his reputation as the one person who could get anything in Lagos preceded him. The only downside was the stingy Papa Omotosho withheld the customary tips, something that the Nneka and Mercy took more personally than Reuben, who found it rather amusing.

One of his errands consisted of driving Papa on the rare occasions when the older man needed to get around. It was interesting that he would let Reuben touch his car, which was covered under a thick tarpaulin sheet, in a revered corner of the compound that no one was allowed to go near. The first time he had driven Papa, it was an exasperating experience, which he narrated to the girls. He had just started driving, and even though he was a confident driver, it was easy for that confidence to be deflated when he was driving Papa Omotosho. Late for his appointment, the older man had instructed Reuben to "hurry up but slow down," and from then on, the older man got the nickname *Papa Hurry Up But Slow Down*.

It was following this incident that Mercy realized that the time had come for her to get her revenge on Papa for having locked them outside the day they had moved into the house. It was a simple plot that they hatched. Reuben was reluctant at first, but the girls had a knack for twisting his arm, and it did not take a long time to convince him. Lilian, of course, was not let in on the plot until the very end. The plan was to have Reuben drive Papa for one of his appointments and stay out late enough that they would arrive after seven, by which time, according to Papa's cardinal rule of security consciousness, the gates of the compound would be padlocked. It seemed like fate had also decided to conspire with them that day because Reuben did not need to make up any of the excuses he had prepared in order to keep them out or take a longer route. A trailer accident had meant that there was a lot of traffic on the way back home. Even Papa could see this himself and remained unusually quiet.

By the time they arrived home, the gates had been padlocked shut as planned. In trying to hide his amazement, Reuben offered to jump over the fence to alert those inside to come out and let them in, to which Papa berated him aggressively and accused him of being a criminal element. It was a sensitive accusation for Reuben, knowing his past, and he waited to hear from Papa what the plan would be.

Papa was a step ahead of him. There was a local hotel nearby, which he told Reuben to drive him to. He checked himself into a room for the night while Reuben spent the entire night in the car with the mosquitoes singing in his ears. Papa had taken the car keys with him to prevent Reuben from driving away.

The next morning the girls prepared for the worst. It was not until it had happened that they had realized the implication of what they had just done, especially when Lilian found out that they had let her father-in-law spend the night outside of his own compound. She had already told the girls to start to prepare to leave the house, calling them ingrates for treating an old man in such a cruel manner as to lock him outside after he had given them all a place to stay, no matter how unpleasant his attitude was.

What happened next shocked them all. Papa returned full of praise for them all. He congratulated them on ensuring that they had obeyed the security rule, which no one, including himself, was above. Stunned into silence, they watched as he left with a spring in his step. They had least expected any praise for their action, and all of them dissolved into laughter as Reuben reminded them that they owed him a ton of favors for what he had just had to endure.

Life was so busy that all this was quickly forgotten. For one thing they were preparing to welcome Adesuwa's little one, who was due to arrive at any moment. Nneka and Mercy had even begun plans to start a children's collection. Their business was expanding quicker than they had imagined possible, and by now they had customers in far-flung parts of the city. They prided themselves on being able to make home deliveries. And when Reuben was not available to do this, they did it themselves. It had been Mercy's idea that they should always take a taxi whenever they had to deliver their clients' clothes. One day they would be able to afford a car, she had said, but until then taxis would be the solution. Even when they were unable to afford the full fare to their destination, they would take a bus to as close as possible to the destination and then take a taxi so they could arrive in style. According to her it made them look less desperate and more professional.

On a particular morning, Nneka felt like walking. She decided it would give her time to reflect on the direction that her life had taken. She had known that she would be making a home delivery that day, and for some reason she had taken some time the day before to meticulously select the clothes she would be wearing. Even as she started walking from the house, having successfully ignored Papa's curious stare as she stepped out of the compound, she knew that she had made a right choice: a loose-fitting dress with a flowery pattern. She felt like she was floating in it, but as she took walked further, she realized that her choice of footwear was not the best. A pair of sandals that were not quite her size. They had been a gift from one of their clients, and although she was grateful at the thoughtfulness of the gesture, she had not realized how uncomfortable they would be. She winced as the heels of her feet grazed the ground. She knew that by the time she reached her destination, the heels of her feet would be bruised and possibly callused, but she kept on walking briskly, in a straight and purposeful manner. There were more important things to worry about.

She should have been tired, as she had stayed up late, putting finishing touches on the outfit she was delivering, and it was not until she was done and had put the *Ariya Couture* tag on it that she felt accomplished. The outfit was now neatly folded in the package she was holding so delicately. The embroidery had been a little tricky, and even Mercy, who was not usually generous with her praise, could not hold it back by the time she was done. She had remarked that even though she had gone to school for this, Nneka was clearly the gifted one.

She smiled, and her eyes wandered to a stray dog walking on the other side of the street. It was clearly female, even though the flesh clung to its bones, the most prominent part of its body was the row of mammary glands that swung from side to side as it sauntered down the road. The slight redness of each swollen nipple was an indication that it had recently birthed a litter of puppies, which were probably somewhere nearby. She watched the dog curiously as it came closer to her. It suddenly wagged its tail happily as it noticed something lying on the road. It went closer and paused to sniff it, but deciding it was not worthwhile, it strutted past Nneka with its tongue dangling from its mouth.

She thought about how that dog, rummaging around in search of something to sustain its survival, was somehow not much different from her and how this vicious cycle would somehow also continue with the newborn puppies as they grew older. At one point in life you come out from under the umbrella of protection that your parents provide and begin to carve out an existence for yourself. She often regretted that hers had happened so unexpectedly, so quickly, and so rudely. She had Aloy to thank for that. Aloy the Philistine! She often wondered what she would do if she ever saw him again.

As she crossed to the other side of the road, she wrinkled her nose as an unpleasant smell was carried through the air by the gentle morning breeze. It was likely that it came from the gutters, and she surveyed her surroundings—the street littered with debris, the rickety planks placed across the gutters leading to the entrances of the homes and the shops.

She did not know if it was fair to place all of this blame on Aloy's doorstep. If only her father had not been so parochial. She had felt so caged, so held back. She had been expected to live her life following a script that she had not been asked to write or comment on. The moment she even attempted to veer off script, she had been discarded like a piece of used clothing that was no longer in fashion. Yes, she could not hide the fact that she was happy. Happier than she could ever had been if she had followed the script. Yes, she missed her parents; she missed Nneoma. She wished that she could have them be a part of this life that she was beginning to carve for herself. She wished that things had turned out differently. She wished she knew where they were. She recalled the betrayal that she had felt when no one had stood up for her. A simple "But Nneka has never stolen anything before!" would have sufficed, but she had been judged and sentenced within a short time. Within the twinkle of an eye, she found herself homeless and alone.

She had thought it would be temporary, that her father would come back to his senses. Everything would be forgiven and forgotten, and it would all be back to normal, whatever normal could be defined as. But days had turned into weeks and weeks into months, and months had gone by, and it was as if she had evaporated into evanescence, almost like she never existed. But in everything she was thankful.

She had had to go through this to realize that family was not always linked by a biological connection. Her real family had forsaken her, but she had gained another family in the process. There was Adesuwa's mom: the indefatigable Mrs. Erhabor, a shining example if there ever was one. What would she have done without her? She had been a guide, a mentor, and most of all, a mother. There was no line demarcating her surrogate children and her own children. She gave everyone equal doses of motherly care and tenderness. There was the mysterious and calm Reuben, who had shown up out of the blue, and now they could not imagine life with him. He had uncanny habit of being able to source those things that they needed, and he did so effortlessly, brushing aside their surprises as if it was one of the easiest things one could do. Reuben's sister Enitanwa had one of the brightest minds that Nneka had ever encountered. She had a sharp memory, something that would serve her well in the future.

She jerked out of her ruminations when she realized that she had walked far enough and needed to look for a taxi so she could arrive at her client's place in style. She found one easily on the busy street and settled into the back seat, proceeding to rub the bottom of her feet as she told the driver her destination. She glanced up as the driver slowed down to let the pedestrians cross the street, and that was when she saw him.

At first she thought she was imagining things because she had just been thinking about him, something she had not done in a long time given the busy pace of her life. But then he also looked into the cab, and their eyes met. He held her stare for a few seconds, and there was a brief pause. She felt her blood run cold through her veins. Aloy. Just like that, there he was. She had never thought she would see him again and had never even planned what she would do if she did.

He looked away and hastened his pace as the taxi driver drove the car away. She watched his retreating figure through the window. She froze. He had disappeared again. All the feelings of hurt and betrayal came rushing back. She had never really had any closure to this episode that had changed her life. She had never told anyone the story of Aloy. Now she had had to relive it all over again.

For the rest of the day, she was a bundle of nerves. No one could understand her sudden silence. Mercy tried to speak with her and was not successful. She buried herself in her work as it was the only outlet she had to retain her sanity. This went on for weeks and then she started to realize that if she did not tell someone, she would actually go insane.

She was alone one day when Reuben came over to the house. He came frequently enough now that he was able to let himself in, and she was so deep in thought that she did not know when he entered the room.

"Let me just start helping myself to what I want," he announced, his usual upbeat self. She gave a weak smile, but then he looked closer at her. "Pardon me saying this, but you look ten years older than you did the last time I saw you."

She did not reply but stared in space

His joviality turned into deep concern as he asked softly, "Nneka, something is wrong—what is making you so sad?" It was the first time anyone had asked her directly. Not Adesuwa, not Mercy, not Lilian. She did not hold it against them; they were close enough that if something was bothering her, it was up to her to let them know.

She looked at Reuben and then looked away. Tears welled up in her eyes as she began. "I saw someone the other day." She sighed heavily. "Someone who…" she stopped. How could she begin to explain her stupidity, her naiveté?

Reuben remained silent and watched her. His face was expression-less—there was neither sympathy nor curiosity in his eyes. There was a slight hint of concern, and that was what made her continue.

She told her story unashamedly, holding nothing back up until the point when she had seen Aloy. When she finished, she felt like a heavy burden had been lifted off her shoulders. She was glad that she had shared this with Reuben and not one of the other girls. She could not explain why. There was just something instinctive about it; it just felt so right. She looked at Reuben, hoping to get some confirmation of what she was feeling.

He was staring at the wall in front of him and now turned to look at her. "Did you say his name is Aloy?"

Made in the USA
Charleston, SC
10 November 2014